DEATH AT ONE BLOW
A SALLY AND JOHNNY HELDAR MYSTERY

HENRIETTA HAMILTON

AGORA BOOKS

ABOUT THE AUTHOR

Henrietta Hamilton is the pseudonym for Hester Denne Shepherd who was born in Dundee in 1920 and was educated at St Hugh's College, Oxford where she earned an honours degree in Modern Languages.

During the Second World War, Hamilton served in the Wrens. Afterwards, she worked in a London bookshop, gaining first-hand experience of antiquarian bookselling — the background of her crime-solving duo, Johnny and Sally Heldar.

During her life, Hamilton enjoyed writing and hill-walking. She died in 1995 in Hastings, East Sussex.

ALSO BY HENRIETTA HAMILTON

THE SALLY AND JOHNNY HELDAR MYSTERIES

The Two Hundred Ghost

Death at One Blow

The Man Who Wasn't There

At Night to Die

Death at Selden End

Cover Her Face

Answer in the Negative

Front for Crime

OTHER NOVELS

The Quarry

Roger Cunningham

Neil and Henrietta

Colin and Sheila

Wrong Turning

The Debateable Land

Lake of Darkness

The Deciding Factor

Hiding the Skeleton

* Italics indicates provisionally named title.

DEATH

AT

ONE BLOW

Copyright © Henrietta Hamilton, 1957

ISBN 978-1-913099-49-7

Cover Design By: Milan Jovanovic

This edition published in 2021 by Agora Books

First published in 1957 by Hodder and Stoughton

Agora Books is a division of Peters Fraser + Dunlop Ltd

55 New Oxford Street, London WC1A 1BS

To
DMM

'It is my belief, Watson, founded upon my experience, that the lowest and vilest alleys in London do not present a more dreadful record of sin than does the smiling and beautiful countryside.'

— Sir Arthur Conan Doyle, *The Copper Beeches*

PROLOGUE

Sally Heldar glanced at her watch. It was five minutes to six. Johnny would be home any time now; after a day like this he would have left the shop as soon as he decently could. It had been hot enough in the flat; in his narrow second-floor office, overlooking the traffic of the Charing Cross Road, it must have been nearly intolerable. It would have been nice to get out of town, but after a month's honeymoon in March and April he couldn't go away again before the autumn.

She went into the kitchen and opened the refrigerator. Johnny would want beer this evening, and she could do with some herself. She collected two bottles and a couple of tumblers, went back to the sitting room, and set the tray down on the rosewood table which had been Uncle Charles Heldar's wedding present. Then she heard Johnny's key in the front door.

He was very tall and broad in the shoulders, with thick brown hair and big features. Sally had never paused to consider whether he was good-looking or not, and in her experience no one else had paused either. There was something in his eyes which took one immediately beyond such considerations: authority, humour, kindness, and a suggestion of other worthwhile things. He gave a general impression of strength and gentleness in equal parts.

He held her very tightly for a moment, as he always did — as if he had been wondering if she mightn't have vanished during his absence. But his kiss was firm and assured. For a few moments neither of them remembered the heat. Then Sally said: 'Beer and then a cold bath, or a cold bath and then beer?'

'Beer first, I think,' said Johnny. 'After that I may have enough energy to get into a bath.' He took off his coat and slung it on to a chair.

When they were sitting on the sofa, he drank deeply and sighed. Then he looked at her and said: 'Would you like to get out of town for a fortnight or so?'

'What — now?'

'Yes. Not a holiday, though it would be a nice change. A job — a rush job.'

Sally understood. 'Somebody's library?'

Johnny nodded, and drank again. 'It's an exceedingly complicated story, and my brain isn't at its best this evening, but I'll try to be lucid. You know old Mercator?'

Sally knew Sir Mark quite well. He had a fine library and, as a partner in one of the biggest firms of merchant bankers in Europe, the means to enlarge it, and he had been a customer of Heldar Brothers for many years. He visited the shop frequently, and in the days when she had worked there had been unfailingly charming and courteous to her. He had always been attached to Johnny and had paid a special call of congratulation when their engagement had appeared in *The Times.* They had dined with him at the Savoy, and he had sent them a fine pair of Queen Anne candlesticks and come as a most welcome guest to their wedding.

Johnny went slowly on. 'I don't know if you knew that his wife was a Thaxton — one of the Hampshire lot. He courted her sometime in the early years of the century, and though money was beginning to come into its own then the Thaxtons had no need of it, and her father stuck in his aristocratic toes at the thought of a Jew. Mercator behaved extremely well — so Grandfather says; I got this bit of gossip from him this afternoon — and spent a year patiently trying to bring the old man round. Then he gave it up and organised a thoroughly business-like and respectable elopement. It was a very successful marriage, and they were both so much liked that they didn't suffer socially. They had no son — only one daughter, who came to a tragic end. She married a German count and ended up in a concentration camp. The Count made trouble about it and disappeared too. There were no children, mercifully. A good many other Mercator connections went the same way, and ultimately Mark was left with only one relative: his late wife's great-nephew, Richard Thaxton.'

'Richard Thaxton,' repeated Sally. 'I've seen that name somewhere. There's the Thaxton Library, of course, isn't there? But I've seen the name quite recently.'

'I expect you have. I'm coming to that. Richard must now be thirtyish. I've never met him, but he had the reputation of being a bit of a waster, and it was said he didn't get on with his father. Anyhow, he stayed on in the RAF after the war, and he was out in Korea, with one of the Sunderland Flying Boat Squadrons, when his old man characteristically broke his neck in the hunting-field. A matter of months after that, Richard himself was shot down. There must have been a certain amount of sheer bad luck in it because a Sunderland isn't easy to shoot down, but at any rate it crashed, and he was reported killed in action. By that time he was an Acting Squadron-Leader, so he must have done extremely well. He had no heir, but he left everything —

9

including the family seat — to his fiancée. I don't know who she is.

'But there had been three deaths within a very short time of each other — Richard's grandfather, another Richard, died at a ripe-ish old age in 'forty-eight — and the fiancée was forced to sell to cover the death duties. This is where Mercator stepped in. He told Grandfather he liked the family seat — it's Westwater Manor, near Fanchester — and he was going to retire from business and was looking round for a country house. He wanted to keep it as nearly as possible in the family, too. Possibly he also wanted to help Richard's girl out. So he bought it, with its contents — I believe there's some beautiful furniture. And, of course, there's the Thaxton Library, collected chiefly by Grandfather Richard. It's a very fine library, as you probably know. There's a 1510 Flambury, among other things, and a First Percival.

'Well, Mercator gradually transferred himself from London to Westwater. He spent a lot of money on the place and made a lot of improvements. He took his own library down and merged it with the Thaxton Library. He intended to have all the books together valued for insurance when he had finally settled in. A month ago he sold his house in Hampstead and went down to Westwater, as he thought, for good and all. Then, two days ago, the Chinese announced that they were magnanimously releasing four RAF men who, they said, had been shot down over Chinese territory while dropping germs. A pretty gesture, of course, in view of the forthcoming Foreign Ministers' Conference. And one of those RAF men, as you have already guessed, is Richard Thaxton.'

Sally took her head in her hands. 'How are they ever going to sort it out?' she asked.

'I'm not a lawyer,' said Johnny, 'thank God. I just

don't know what happens, but I imagine it's a quite incredibly complicated business. Mercifully it's all in the family, so to speak. Mercator's one idea is to help Richard back to his own, and he says that Westwater is of course Richard's home from the moment he gets back, which will probably be in another fortnight or three weeks. Which is where we come in. Mercator wants to get the two libraries sorted out, and that's more or less a skilled job. He's never used a book plate, and there's no Thaxton plate either, so there's no simple means of distinguishing the books. It's got to be done from the catalogues, and it'll be a bit tricky here and here. Mercator could do it himself, but his eyesight isn't very good, and anyway he's rushing about dealing with lawyers and trying to communicate with Richard. So we've got to take it on. What's more, he wants both the libraries revalued for insurance at the same time, so as to get the whole job over at once. He got Richard's authority to have the Thaxton Library revalued before Richard was shot down. And he wants it all done before Richard gets back. That's understandable; he wouldn't want people in the house at that time.

'Well, if it had been almost anyone else, we'd have said we couldn't do it at such short notice, in the middle of the holiday season. But Mercator is such a valued customer and such an old friend that we felt we'd got to oblige him. Now, Grandfather can't get away, and Uncle Charles is in Cornwall, so I've got to take it on. But I've got to have help if I'm to do it in the time — it's a very big job. We talked it over with Mercator, and it was finally agreed that you should be asked to come down with me. He's asked us both to go as his guests, and I think it ought to be rather fun. Is it all right with you?'

'Very much so,' said Sally. 'But is it really all right with the firm? I'm not on the staff any longer.'

'Would you rather I took Miss Jennings?' asked Johnny solemnly.

'Would you like to take Miss Jennings, darling?'

Johnny shrugged his shoulders. 'Well, it would be a change, wouldn't it?'

'You brute,' said Sally.

Johnny grinned. 'I could take her, but she wouldn't be nearly as good as you. From any point of view. So I think you'd better come. You get your old salary, by the way.'

'For living in the lap of luxury, and...and working with you?'

'You've never worked with me yet. You may find you simply loathe it.'

'There's always that,' said Sally.

CHAPTER ONE

They drove down to Westwater two days later. The weather had shown no sign of breaking, and it was a tremendous relief to get away. Johnny drove as fast as the Sunday traffic allowed, and they were cool for almost the first time in three weeks.

Just after half-past three they rose up to a high, bare shoulder, and saw a little valley lying below them like a deep green pocket in the downs. Its floor was an oval of parkland. A little river ran down the east side, and lay in silver links at the farther end, where they could see a tiny village. That, Johnny said, would be Danesfield. Almost in the centre of the park, with a glimpse of gardens beyond, was the mellow brick of a great house.

They took a side road which dropped steeply down the slopes, and presently came to open lodge gates with high grey pillars topped by recumbent stone lions. The lodge was a little square eighteenth-century cottage standing in a garden thick with stocks and late roses. Then there was a long, well-kept avenue lined with beeches, and beyond them the sunlit stretches of the park.

They didn't see the house until they were round the last bend. They discovered later that its south front was more impressive but seen as they approached it from the North it was still extraordinarily lovely. It was built round three sides of a courtyard, into which they were now looking. The two wings had been extended, as they knew, in the nineteenth-century, but the work had been so well done that it had blended into the original Georgian building until it was almost impossible to distinguish one from the other. The proportions still seemed perfect; the pillared porch retained its quiet dignity, and the flagged court was still spacious. In the centre of it rose a mulberry tree which must have been as old as the original house.

Johnny had slowed down for a moment so that they could both look. Now he drove on between the wide green lawns. In front of the house there was a broad sweep of gravel from which the avenue branched to right and left. The gravel led them on to the flags of the courtyard, and Johnny turned and stopped before the great front door.

As they were leaving the car, an impressive butler appeared in the open doorway. He was in the act of taking charge of them when Mercator's thin, friendly voice said: 'So here you are!'

He came down the steps, a small, slender, white-haired figure in flannels, with a dignity and authority which were always faintly surprising until he began to talk. The last time they had seen him he had had the pallor of the city-dweller; now the sun had browned him a little, and the slight tan suited his fine features — even the nose, which just betrayed his race, had a curious delicacy about it. His dark eyes were shining with pleasure behind his spectacles.

'My dear Mrs Heldar, I'm delighted to see you.' He had been born and brought up in England, and his clear, precise speech had no hint of accent. 'Heldar, this is very nice. It's exceedingly good of you both to have come.' His small, thin hand clasped theirs in turn. 'Such weather! We might almost be in southern Italy. Come along in. You'll want to see your room, and then we'll have tea in the drawing room. The terrace is really too hot before evening.'

He led them through a marble-floored vestibule, where a carved choir stall stood on either side, and into a great hall. Opposite them a double staircase rose to two long galleries, with a high window above it. Sally lost the thread of what Mercator was saying and came to herself in a sudden silence.

'I'm so sorry, Sir Mark,' she said quickly. 'I had to stare.'

Mercator smiled. 'Yes,' he said. 'I have seen a good many of the great houses of England, and I have always thought this the most beautiful. I should have been a little hurt if you hadn't stared.'

He took them up one curved flight of the magnificent staircase, and along a gallery to a corridor which ran on the courtyard side. Then he showed them a big, sunlit bedroom, its walls hung with an old white brocade, and the two tall windows curtained with powder blue.

'I hope you'll find yourselves comfortable,' he said. 'And here are Emmanuel and Annie, who will look after you.'

Emmanuel, who had appeared in the doorway of the dressing room, was a slight, olive-skinned, elderly valet, whose race was written far more plainly in his face than in his master's. Annie was a plump, fresh-faced country woman, obviously a trained servant, but too pleasant and homely to worry Sally, who had seldom been provided with a maid. She found herself delighted by the lovely room, the old walnut furniture, the formal garden with its roses and violas beyond the windows.

Mercator was waiting for them in the hall and led them along a corridor to the drawing room. It was a long, high room in a corner of the house, with windows opening on to a terrace on the South, and lawns divided by one of the avenues on the West. The walls were ivory, and the curtains a yellow so pale that it was almost white. The brocaded furniture was ivory too, with here and there a vivid cushion. There were flowers everywhere, making more splashes of bright colour. It was an exquisite room, created with a taste that was almost feminine, yet not effeminate. Sally, staring again, decided that it was a fairly accurate reflection of Mercator. A quiet, traditionally conventional background, with flashes of eccentricity which might very easily have been in the worst of expensive bad taste but were in fact delightful. She noticed something else, too. The room might very easily have been a showroom, frozen into a Sleeping Beauty trance a hundred and fifty years ago, wanting only a red velvet cordon to keep visitors from touching its beautiful furniture. But it wasn't. It was habitable, with a friendly atmosphere of habitation.

They sat down round the white Adam fireplace. Lawrence's portrait of Elizabeth Thaxton, the famous Regency beauty, hung above it, and an enormous vase of carmine gladioli stood in the tiled hearth. Sally was looking at the fascinating Elizabeth when the door opened, and a young man came in. He was the first person she had seen who was entirely out of keeping with the house.

He was tallish, but his stooped, narrow shoulders detracted from his height. He was angular and rather awkward in his movements, and his crumpled flannels didn't quite fit him. His black hair was lank, but a little untidy, and his pale face was disfigured by a pair of horn-rimmed spectacles with immensely thick lenses.

He looked, thought Sally, like a student from a provincial university, but as soon as the thought had crossed her mind, she reproached herself for her snobbishness, for there was something rather pathetic about him.

Mercator introduced him. 'Mrs Heldar, this is Cecil Deane, my secretary.'

Deane shook hands limply and mumbled something half intelligible. Then he greeted Johnny, stumbled over a footstool, and sat down ungracefully on one of the brocaded chairs.

The butler brought in tea, and Mercator asked Sally to pour out. The teapot was Georgian silver, and the china Coalport. Deane got to his feet and handed cups and plates, and she found herself praying silently that he wouldn't drop the priceless pieces. But through her appreciation and her anxiety she was aware that Mercator was watching her as she sat behind the tea tray. She was a little puzzled by his quiet observation, but she knew that it was essentially kind.

After a minute or two he spoke again. His table-talk was charming, inconsequential, and witty, and he never monopolised the conversation. Johnny and Sally found it quite easy to meet him half-way. But Deane, in spite of occasional efforts to draw him, sat almost silent. He was obviously out of place in this setting, and perhaps, Sally thought, painfully conscious of it. She guessed at first that he hadn't been long with Mercator, who might well have acquired a private secretary only after his retirement. It surprised her a little to hear that he had been with Sir Mark for three years. But perhaps Westwater was a different cup of tea to the house in Hampstead. As soon as they had finished, he excused himself and left the drawing room.

Presently Mercator said he would like to take the

Heldars over the house, and they went out into the corridor.

The principal rooms were all in the central block, opening on to the terrace. Next to the drawing room was the library, a big square room lined with books to within three feet of the high ceiling. Sally was a little appalled by the extent of the job which lay before them, but Johnny seemed to take it quite calmly. Next to the library was the hall, and down the corridor on the farther side was Mercator's study, a pleasant room, workmanlike but not functional, with a solid writing table and some old wing chairs. Above the mantelpiece was the portrait of a young girl. Her face was a clear-cut oval against a dark background, with delicate features and a fine, pale skin, and her blue eyes were gentle and full of laughter. Her hair was a soft russet, like beech leaves in autumn. There was a fleeting resemblance to Mercator himself, and Sally identified her just as he said: 'That is my daughter. Sargent's portrait.'

'She is lovely,' said Sally. It seemed the only thing to say.

Mercator smiled, and looked at Johnny. 'Yes. She is lovely,' he said.

Beyond the study, in the south-east corner, was the dining room, and next door, in the east wing, the morning room. The east wing proper was the servants' quarters. Mercator explained that he had no house-keeper, since he preferred to order his own dinner, and was therefore at liberty to wander about his kitchens as the spirit moved him. It was here that his renovations were most apparent. Every possible modern amenity which could make his servants' lives easier seemed to have been provided, and it was perfectly clear that the servants were appreciative. Even the French chef, muttering over some concoction on the big electric cooker,

18

was obviously both accustomed and delighted to see his master.

They looked at the west wing, with the estate office and the nineteenth-century smoking room and gun room. Then they went upstairs and saw the picture gallery and some of the other first-floor rooms. Finally Mercator took them out to the stables on the east side of the house, and showed them his conversions there, and when they returned the dressing gong was sounding.

Sally was doing her face when Johnny wandered back from their private bathroom. He came over to her, and they smiled at each other in the mirror.

'Very nice,' he said. 'But not quite so cosy as the flat.'

'No,' said Sally gravely.

Johnny asked abruptly: 'Does it worry you that I can't give you this sort of thing?'

'Worry me? *Worry* me?'

'All right,' said Johnny, with an absurd relief in his voice. 'I just wanted to be sure.'

* * *

OCCASIONALLY THE HELDARS had a special evening out, but they agreed afterwards that they had never eaten a better dinner than Mercator's. The French chef was obviously one of his most priceless possessions. So was his Burgundy. The Westwater dining room made a worthy background, and Mercator himself was at his wittiest and most charming. Sally was only sorry to observe that Deane remained unaffected by these influences. He was as silent as he had been at tea, and as soon as they had drunk Antoine's exquisite coffee and Mercator's cognac, he mumbled his excuses and good nights and went away.

Mercator took the Heldars out for a little while, to

walk in the formal garden, and then, having discovered in the course of the evening that they shared his interest in music, brought them back to the drawing room and opened a big Sheraton cabinet which held gramophone records.

'Perhaps you'll choose one,' he said. 'My sight isn't as good as it was.'

After a little discussion Johnny chose the *Variations on the St Anthony Passion* and put it on the big radiogram, and they settled down to listen.

They had been listening for about five minutes when they were rudely interrupted. A heavy step sounded on the terrace, and as Sally looked up a short, stout, brick-red gentleman in a dinner jacket appeared at the open French window and charged into the room like an excited bull.

'Ah!' he shouted. 'So there you are, Mercator! You got my letter?'

'Indeed, yes,' said Mercator mildly. 'Come in, my friend; come in. I am delighted to see you.'

This invitation seemed to excite the visitor even further. He turned a rather deeper red. 'Well?' he demanded truculently. Then he followed Mercator's reproachful glance to Sally and made her a slight bow. 'I beg your pardon, madam.'

There was a gleam of amusement in Mercator's eye. 'Mrs Heldar, permit me to present Colonel Danby, my neighbour — but, alas, not for long!'

'That's just it!' shouted the Colonel triumphantly. Then he remembered Sally's presence, hastily lowered his voice, and acknowledged Mercator's introduction. Johnny, who had risen, was then presented. The Colonel gave him just as much time as bare civility demanded, and then turned upon Mercator again.

'Ah, yes, my dear friend,' said Mercator. 'Your letter—'

Sally murmured: 'If you want to talk business, Sir Mark, perhaps we might look at the library.'

'But no!' said Mercator. 'Indeed no, my dear Mrs Heldar. You and your husband will stay and see fair play, as the British say.'

Sally's suspicion that he was playing up to the Colonel became more marked, and she sat down again. She glanced at Johnny, and his solemn expression was as good as a wink.

'Well, if you insist,' said the Colonel huffily.

'But of course. I am at your service. Sit down; sit down. Excuse me while I turn off the radio gramophone. I know that you do not care for music.'

He came back, sat down, and smiled charmingly and attentively at the Colonel.

'Well?' said Danby. 'What are you going to do about it? 'The note of triumph was back in his voice.

Mercator shrugged his shoulders and spread out his hands. The gesture was very successful.

'Dammit, sir!' roared the Colonel. Then he turned hurriedly to Sally. 'Beg your pardon, Mrs Heldar.' He went on, keeping his voice down with an agonising effort. 'There's only one thing you can do, as I told you in my letter. I'd have come as soon as I heard the news of Richard if I hadn't been in Scotland. Stop building your dam — beastly farm. You can't build on another man's land, sir. And if you try, I shall take action. Now that Richard's alive, it's a very different kettle of fish.' He rubbed his fat hands together with satisfaction.

'You think so?' asked Mercator deprecatingly.

'I know, sir! I'm a Justice of the Peace. You'll have to stop building. And as soon as Richard gets back, he'll have your filthy erection pulled down. Spoiling the view for miles and ruining my reach of the river. The fish will never come up with your blasted dam across the water. Richard will never allow that. He's got too much feeling for the countryside, and too much consideration for his neighbours.'

'But it would be such a pity!' cried Mercator. 'My beautiful buildings — they are nearly finished. I shall most certainly advise Richard to preserve them. If the farm is properly run, it will bring him in a great deal of money.'

The Colonel forgot Sally and Johnny, and his parade ground voice shook the Chelsea figures on the mantelpiece. He raved incoherently on the subjects of rural amenities and riparian rights. Mercator listened to him for a little, and then flew into a Continental rage. He used every trick of expression and gesture, and he hurled insults in several languages. Sally noticed, however, that whether the Colonel knew it or not the insults were more picturesque than damaging, and not one of them embarrassed her in the smallest degree. She enjoyed the proceedings until the Colonel and Mercator got on their feet, and the Colonel began to look dangerous. Then she glanced at Johnny again. But Johnny had stood up too.

'Gentlemen, gentlemen,' he said apologetically. Sally thought he was going to remind them that there was a lady present but evidently he balked at that. In any case it wasn't necessary. Mercator fizzled out at once. The Colonel turned a furious face on Johnny, opened his mouth for another bellow, and then shut it again.

'I beg your pardon,' he said abruptly. 'Quite right, my boy.' He turned to Sally again. 'Beg your pardon, Mrs Heldar. Inexcusable behaviour. I hope you weren't frightened.'

Sally managed to bow to him. He nodded stiffly to Mercator and said: 'We'll discuss this another time. Good night.' Then he turned and marched out by the window, and they heard his footsteps die away on the terrace.

'Mrs Heldar,' said Mercator, 'I owe you an apology too, though I'm not going to ask you if you were frightened. But I can't resist Danby, and he does love a good row.'

'Almost as much as you do,' said Sally, and smiled at him.

He smiled back at her with amusement and something that was almost like affection. 'How right you are, my dear! 'he said. 'And how well-timed and how masterly your husband's intervention was!' He sighed. 'I don't think he'll be able to see more than one gable of my farm from his house, and I don't think it will be in the least offensive — that is, if Richard decides to finish it. And I've made a by-pass for the fish to go up. I took expert advice, and the plans were passed, so I damn well know — my apologies, madam, but more for the inevitable pun than for the language — that my dam won't affect his fishing. But he refuses to believe it, and of course it would be very dull if he did. Well, well. Let us have the record on again.'

When the Brahms was finished, Johnny put on Bach's *Sheep May Safely Graze*. Peace had returned to the lovely room; Sally lay back in her chair and looked at Johnny, sitting on the sofa, and saw that he was looking at her. Then again, almost without a sound this time, the peace was shattered.

She became aware of another presence in the room and looked up to see a young man standing in one of the windows. For a moment he stood so still that she almost wondered if Westwater had a ghost. But he was no Thaxton ghost, at any rate, if the family portraits could be taken as a guide. His hair was fair, but not the almost inevitable red. He had once been good-looking, but he could never have had the Thaxton perfection of feature. His face was pale, and curiously haggard, and Sally wondered if he were ill. Then he spoke, and the thick voice gave her the clue. He might be ill — he had probably been drinking long enough to make him.

'So there you are,' he said. He spoke quite quietly, but his quietness was a good deal more disturbing than the Colonel's shout.

Mercator stood up. 'Forgive me, Mrs Heldar,' he said. 'Yes, here I am, Willesdon. If you want to talk to me, I think we'd better go along to my study.'

'Oh, no.' The voice was still quiet, but the young man came a couple of paces into the room, staggering a little. 'Oh, no. We'll have witnesses in on this scene.'

'I've asked you to come to my study,' said Mercator steadily.

'Like a naughty boy seeing the headmaster?' The voice rose slightly. 'No, thanks very much, Mercator. We'll have this out on the spot. I want my job back, and I want it now. Things will be different, you know, now Dick's coming home. He'll give me my job back if you don't. So you'd much better take me back now and avoid any more unpleasantness.' He lunged forward again, and his look was ugly.

Mercator didn't move. 'Heldar,' he said, 'will you please take your wife into the library?'

'I will, sir,' said Johnny. 'And then I'll come back if you don't mind.'

'Perhaps it would be a good idea. Thank you.'

'Damn good idea,' said the young man. 'I'll have a witness. And he doesn't look like a dirty Jew, either.'

Sally felt Johnny's hand tighten sharply on her arm. But he said nothing. He led her out of the room and into the library.

'Be careful,' she said. Rather absurdly, she knew, because Johnny could give a couple of stone to the young man in the drawing room, and he was always fighting fit. What was more, he had been a Commando.

He looked down at her for a second, big and reassuring. He was a little white, which in a Heldar was a sign of anger, but he smiled at her. 'Not to worry,' he said, and went out.

The walls were thick, and for what seemed a long time Sally heard nothing at all. Then Willesdon's voice was raised in obvious protest on the terrace. There was a slight scuffling sound, and then nothing more.

A few minutes later Johnny came back. His colour was normal again, and he wasn't even dishevelled. When she looked enquiringly at him, he said: 'Not now. Come on, darling.'

Mercator was standing on the hearthrug. 'This time, Mrs Heldar,' he said, 'I do owe you an apology. I'm very sorry indeed that you should have been involved in such an unpleasant incident. I can only say that, thanks to your husband, I don't think it will be repeated.'

* * *

JOHNNY CAME in from the dressing room in his pyjamas and joined Sally on the low window seat. Both the windows were open, and the scent of night flowers drifted in.

'I think I can tell you what the fun and games were all about,' he said. 'Willesdon was an RAF buddy of Richard's. He finished his term a few months before Richard went to Korea, and after old Thaxton broke his neck Richard appointed him land-agent here. The old agent was retiring. It was obviously a damn silly thing to do; I gather he knew nothing whatever about running an estate, and he isn't even a countryman. When Mercator came to look into things, he found that Willesdon was three-parts tight for most of the time, and hopelessly incompetent even when he was sober. So he sacked him. He hasn't taken on anyone else; he likes running the place himself, and I should think he's

25

quite good at it. I imagine Willesdon didn't dare to take the matter up until he heard Richard was alive, and then he had to get well primed with gin before he felt able to come down — he's in London now, I understand. It's up to Richard, of course, but he'll be a fool if he takes the man back.'

'What did you do to him?'

'I kicked him down the terrace steps if you must know. I'm sorry, duckie — it was a very nasty little scene for you.'

'Not to worry,' said Sally. 'I must say I enjoyed the Colonel.'

Johnny laughed. 'That was a wicked act of Mercator's. The flowery and excitable foreigner, with a touch of the dilettante and a hint of the commercial — nothing could have been better calculated to arouse the Colonel's wrath. Danby's a period piece, of course; I didn't know they still existed.'

'I rather like him,' said Sally thoughtfully. 'And I love Mercator.'

'Do you know why Mercator loves you, darling? He told me at the shop last week that you're like his daughter.'

'His daughter? I've got the same hair, more or less, but surely that's all. I mean, she was really lovely.'

'Really lovely,' said Johnny gravely. 'Her portrait is very like you.'

CHAPTER TWO

The Heldars breakfasted in their room and were in the library before nine o'clock. They were faced with a long job which would be fairly straightforward in parts, and extremely complicated in others. Mercator's cataloguing of his own books was almost professional in its accuracy, and right up to date. The Thaxton Library was not so easy. Grandfather Richard had had a catalogue printed in 1937 but the numerous acquisitions he had made since then were represented only by a profusion of notes in his own crabbed hand, which became steadily less accurate and intelligible towards the end of his life. There was also a certain number of sporting books — the only literary interest of his son James — which were not mentioned anywhere at all. Finally, Mercator had meticulously arranged all the books according to periods, authors, and subjects, until all apparent distinction between the two libraries seemed hopelessly lost.

But Johnny had a gift for bringing order out of chaos with the least possible trouble and mess. 'First,' he said firmly, 'we must get a working knowledge of Mercator's arrangement of the books, so that we know where to look for what we want. Come on.'

He had an enormous knowledge and a very quick eye, and they moved round the room slowly, but still at a pace which surprised Sally, while he pointed out various authors and categories. Occasionally they indulged themselves so far as to stop and look at some particularly interesting book. They saw the Latin Grammar printed by Helsingheim in 1493, and the 1510 Flambury. Then Johnny paused a moment to look for the First Edition of Percival's *Garland for Gloriana*. It wasn't so rare as either of the other two, but as a courtier's gift of poetry to an ageing queen it had an historical as well as a purely romantic interest.

'Yes, here it is,' he said, looking at the faded gilt lettering on the spine. 'Eighteenth-century calf; that's right.' He opened the book, and then seemed to quicken to a sharper attention. 'Sally, this is damn funny. Look.'

Sally looked at the title page. The light from one of the tall windows fell full on it.

'Someone's altered the date,' she said. 'It's been made to read "1588" — the date of the First Edition.'

'That's right,' said Johnny. 'It's a clumsy attempt at forgery.' He held the page up to the light. 'Yes. This is the reprint of 1675. You can see the original figures underneath. They'd be comparatively easy to alter. And this is seventeenth-century paper. Otherwise the title page is practically the same as the title page of the First — similar print, and the same lay-out. And for some reason no printer's name.' He was frowning slightly.

'What does it mean?' asked Sally.

'I hope it simply means that either Grandfather Richard or Mercator bought this as a freak and a mildly entertaining monument to human frailty. It would be worth anything up to three pounds if it weren't defaced. But I shan't be quite happy until we find the First.'

They looked all through the shelf on which the reprint had stood, and they cleared out all the books on it and looked behind them. Then they searched the surrounding shelves. Then they searched the catalogues and Grandfather Richard's notes, but there was no record of the reprint.

'This is not conclusive,' said Johnny slowly. 'The First may conceivably be anywhere in this room, and it's perfectly possible that the reprint wasn't taken seriously enough to be catalogued. But I don't like this, Sally. The forgery is comparatively recent — within the last few years, anyway. An expert would be able to get nearer the date, of course. In any case, I doubt if anyone would have tried this on in Grandfather Richard's day; he'd have spotted it too quickly. Besides, the library was valued for probate after his death, and a thing like this couldn't have been overlooked. But it wasn't revalued after his son's death, or after Richard's supposed death; the last valuation was accepted, since it was so recent.'

'Then who...?'

'That's a perfectly horrible question. Not a servant, almost certainly; they wouldn't have the requisite knowledge. And one can't quite see James doing it.'

They looked at each other, and Sally said unhappily: 'Richard?'

'It's possible, I'm afraid, though by no means certain. Richard was said to be a waster; he was said to be on bad terms with his father; his father was said to keep him pretty short of money. And from what I know of James, he never opened a book, apart from sporting volumes, from one year's end to another, and if he had opened the reprint, he mightn't have realised anything was wrong. Richard can't have done this since his father's death, of course, because he hasn't been home.'

'Could Richard have sold the First?' Selling rare books as stolen goods was a very chancy business, because any well-informed and honest antiquarian bookseller was liable to suspect the provenance of a volume and ask awkward questions.

'Well, I should have thought it was doubtful, though the Percival isn't as rare as all that. It was presented to the Queen in manuscript — the manuscript is now in the States — but quite a lot of copies were printed afterwards. I suppose it flattered her vanity, so she didn't object. But it does begin to look as if someone had managed to sell the thing, and Richard might have had as good a chance as anyone. He wasn't known in the trade, and if he didn't give his own name and told a good story he might have got away with it. He'd get up to a hundred pounds for it, and if he was in debt that could come in quite handy. It's not an awful lot, though. I hope to God we don't find any more substitutions.'

'The alternative is,' said Sally, 'that some visiting collector coveted it and stole it from James for himself. I doubt if James entertained collectors in the ordinary way, but with a famous library he might have got them wished on him.'

'That's certainly an idea,' said Johnny. 'It's quite possible, and I hope you're right. But I'm afraid we'll have to tell Mercator about this.'

Mercator had sent a message by Fenton, the butler, to say that he proposed to give himself the pleasure of joining them for coffee at eleven o'clock. He took Johnny's report very quietly, and then pulled out a powerful magnifying glass and looked at the title page of the reprint.

'To be perfectly honest,' he said, 'I can't make anything of it. My sight has deteriorated a good deal lately. But of course you must be right.' He sighed a little. 'Well, this is rather distressing. If the First doesn't turn up, you'll just have to delete it from the catalogue. And you'd better omit this...this curiosity.' He touched the reprint lightly, and then tucked it under his arm and rose.

'I think he suspects Richard too,' said Sally when he had gone. 'If he didn't, he wouldn't have refused to discuss it.'

'I'm afraid you're right. If the prodigal son chose to take part of his portion in advance, there's nothing to be done about it now he's come into the rest. It's none of our business, anyway.'

* * *

AT TWENTY TO ONE they knocked off. Johnny took off his dustcoat and Sally her overall, and they went upstairs to wash. Then they joined Mercator in the drawing room, and a minute or two later Deane appeared. He seemed even more silent than usual.

Fenton was announcing lunch when they heard a car draw up outside the open front door. Mercator said: 'See who it is, Fenton. We'll wait a minute.'

He was talking appreciatively about the Heldars' wedding when the door opened again. Fenton announced, with a suspicion of excitement in his normally expressionless voice: 'Miss Harz and Mr Richard, sir.'

The girl was extraordinarily attractive. Not beautiful, not pretty, but with a face at which even Sally was compelled to look, and a strange appealing quality. The face was small and heart-shaped, with soft hollows under the cheekbones, a tiny, upturned nose, and a wide mouth that was at the same time gay and a little sad. The eyes were wide and grey. The girl's hair was very fair, and softly waved, and she wore a ridiculous hat with great success. She was small, and her figure was quite perfect. Her printed silk frock was entirely simple and entirely smart. It was the frock which gave

Sally the final clue. The name and the face had been vaguely familiar. This was Lisa Harz, the German model, who was seen in exquisite, simple frocks in all the leading fashion magazines.

The young man who followed her, towering over her in his uniform, was unmistakably a Thaxton. He had the classic features, the thick, curly red hair, and the lean height. But his face under the flaming hair had an almost shocking pallor, and the skin was stretched tight over the fine bones. As he moved up beside the girl, Sally saw that his body was skeleton-thin.

She looked at Mercator, who was just rising, and caught a strange expression in his face. It was as if he had received a sudden shock. That wasn't surprising in itself, but he looked as if the shock were not entirely a pleasurable one. Then she remembered the Percival. But there was no doubt about his pleasure when he said: 'Richard, my boy!' and strode forward with his hands outstretched.

Richard Thaxton moved to meet him and took his hands quickly and a little awkwardly. He towered over Mercator now, looking down at him with a tight, twisted smile. Sally saw affection in his face, almost tenderness. But she realised that he couldn't stand much more of this.

Mercator realised it too. To his great credit he let Richard's hands go and said with his usual mild friendliness: 'This is delightful, Richard. But I didn't expect you for another ten days at least. How did you manage it?'

'I hitched,' said Richard. His voice was taut, but steady. 'Thumbed air-lifts, so to speak.'

'Ah, yes. The RAF has a remarkable gift for ignoring red tape.'

'I got to London yesterday afternoon,' Richard continued, 'and went straight to Lisa.' He spoke the last

32

words with a simplicity curiously at variance with the
painful look of experience in his eyes: the simplicity of
a man deeply in love. His haggard face took on a sort of
luminous happiness. After a moment he went on: 'And
today we thought we'd come down and see you. Lisa's
taking three weeks' holiday.'

'Very nice of you, my boy. And it's a great pleasure
to see Miss Harz again.' He shook hands with the girl,
and then turned.

'Mrs Heldar, I know you'll forgive us. Let me intro-
duce my great-nephew, Richard Thaxton, and his fiancée, Miss Harz. Richard, Mr and Mrs Heldar have
been kind enough to come down to sort out our re-
spective libraries, which I had prematurely mixed up.'

Richard shook hands with Sally, and gave her, suddenly, a charming smile. 'I don't envy you that job,' he
said.

Lunch was a great deal easier than it might have
been. Mercator had up a bottle of the claret he had
brought from Hampstead, but he did not attempt to
propose Richard's health, and he behaved exactly as if
Richard had come home on a normal leave. Lisa was
gay and warm, and very happy to have Richard back,
but she was neither intense nor sentimental. With Mercator and the Heldars she was very friendly, and she
even managed to awake some response in Deane. With
this support Richard did very well. His voice was
slightly brittle at times, and his hands shook a little, but
he managed to carry the situation off. But it was clear
that he would need very careful handling for a long
time. On her present showing, Lisa was probably capable of that. Sally saw now that she was older than she
appeared at a first glance. There was something experienced in her eyes as well as in Richard's. Since she was
German, her experience also might have been painful.
She was probably older than Richard — though at the

moment he looked years older than she did. But that might be quite a good thing.

As soon as they decently could, Sally and Johnny went back to their work. Johnny shut the library door behind them and sighed.

'My God!' he said. 'Well, it might have been worse, and I suppose we helped to keep the temperature down. Though I think Mercator and the girl could have managed quite well without us.'

'I suppose we stay? I gather they're only down for the day.'

'We'll have a word with Mercator when they've gone, but I should think we stay.'

They worked steadily through the early afternoon. In spite of their slightly embarrassing situation, Sally was ridiculously happy. They worked extraordinarily well together, foreseeing each other's wants, conversing or dictating in the peculiar shorthand speech of two people in the same trade, but needing even fewer words because their minds worked so closely together. They were so completely concentrated as to be aware of nothing but their work and one another, and when the cry rang out suddenly in the hall it took them a moment or two to orientate themselves. Then Johnny put down the book he had been holding and ran to the door.

Sally followed him. She saw Fenton standing by the nearer flight of the staircase, and Emmanuel kneeling on the parquet floor. They were both bent over Mercator, who was lying very still, with his head almost under the table which stood between the flights.

* * *

THE TWO SERVANTS drew back a little before Johnny's quiet authority, and he knelt down beside Mercator and looked closely at him. Emmanuel said suddenly: 'I think he has had a stroke,' and though his voice was low it had a strange weeping quality that seemed almost as old as time.

'Perhaps,' said Johnny. 'But it looks as if the rug had slipped under him.' He indicated the long strip of Chinese carpet which had slid out of its place in front of the table. Then he ran his fingers very gently over the thick, low-growing hair above Mercator's forehead. 'He's had a bad blow; he must have hit his head on the edge of the table. Where's the nearest doctor?'

'In the village, sir.' Fenton's voice trembled a little. 'Sir Mark's own man is in Harley Street, but Dr Hill is said to be very good, sir.'

'Ring him up and ask him to come at once. If he's not at home, try to send a message. I suppose Mr Richard and Miss Harz are still here?'

'I don't know, sir. I haven't been to the drawing room.'

'Sally,' said Johnny, 'go and tell them. Emmanuel, go ahead of me and open the door of Sir Mark's room.' He bent down and picked up Mercator as easily as if the old man had been a child.

Sally tried the drawing room and the terrace and ran all round the garden before she thought of seeing if Richard's car was still there. Annoyed by her own stupidity, she ran back and looked into the courtyard. Except for the mulberry tree, it was quite empty.

The doctor arrived a few minutes later — a grey-haired, middle-aged man who seemed reassuringly competent. He appeared to think that Mercator hadn't had a stroke, but he was obviously anxious. He briefly discussed the question of hospital, nursing home, or leaving Mercator where he was, and accepted, subject to the approval of Sir Mark's Harley Street man, Emmanuel's earnest assurance that his master would far rather be ill at home. In the meantime he would get hold of two nurses. Before he went downstairs to telephone, he told Johnny, whose temporary authority he seemed, like the servants, to have accepted, that Richard had better be brought back.

For an hour or so Sally sat in Mercator's room, first with Johnny, while Dr Hill telephoned, and then with Dr Hill, while Johnny telephoned. No one appeared to know when Richard and Lisa had left, but three o'clock seemed the earliest time that was at all likely, and Johnny started on the number of the only Lisa Harz in the London Telephone Directory — of which Mercator had a copy — at about a quarter to five. Richard was staying at his club, but it seemed better to let Lisa break the news to him. Johnny got no reply until a quarter to six, by which time Sally had joined him, for a nurse had arrived from Fanchester. They sat in the little telephone room to the left of the front door, and Johnny told Lisa what had happened.

'They're starting back at once,' he said at last, putting down the receiver and wiping his brow. 'Richard's with her, as you must have gathered. They left here at a quarter to four — which must have been just before it happened — and got in about ten minutes ago.'

'A little odd that they left just before tea.'

'Perhaps they had to get back by half-past five. Or perhaps Richard just felt he couldn't stay any longer.'

'I take it we go when they get back?'

'Yes, I think so. We must hand over to them. We seem to have been taking charge a bit coolly in another man's house, but we couldn't do anything else. The servants are pretty helpless, and Deane is a dead loss. He just sits in his room and jitters. Well, let's go and clear up the library.'

Just before seven, when they were packing, Emmanuel came to Johnny's dressing room with better news. Mercator had recovered consciousness. But Hill was keeping him very quiet, and there seemed to be no certainty that the danger was past. About a quarter past seven the Harley Street man arrived, and at a quarter to eight, while he was still upstairs, Richard and Lisa got back.

Richard listened attentively to Johnny's further explanations, but he looked desperately harassed. He had himself under control, but only just. A quarter of an hour later Fenton came to say that the doctors were in the morning room, and he excused himself and went to see them.

Fenton, perhaps because he was pulling himself together, or perhaps from force of habit, brought in drinks, for which they were all thankful. But another quarter of an hour passed before Richard reappeared.

'They're being cagey, of course,' he said wearily. 'Doctors can never say yes or no to anything. I think it boils down to the fact that they're more hopeful since he recovered consciousness, but they're still pretty worried. Thank you, darling.' He took a glass from Lisa. 'I gather they think he's just got concussion, but they won't rule out the possibility of a fracture. He must have been putting out some letters for the post when the rug skidded under him. That floor is very highly polished. He asked for me, and they let me see him for about two minutes. He looks pretty bad. They didn't want him to talk, but he told me' — Richard turned to the Heldars — 'he'd be grateful if you'd stay on. I hope you will too. God knows who this house belongs to at the moment' — he smiled his astonishingly attractive smile — 'but we both seem to feel that you're an asset.'

CHAPTER THREE

The shadow of anxiety was lifted sooner than anyone had expected. For a man of seventy-two who had suffered a comparatively severe concussion, Mercator made an astonishingly quick recovery. His accident had taken place on Monday afternoon. He took things very quietly on Tuesday, and saw no one but Richard, and him only for a few minutes. But on Wednesday and Thursday he was defying his nurses, sitting up, and demanding solid food. On Friday he ordered Richard and Lisa back to town, telling them to go and amuse themselves, and that afternoon the doctors threw in their hand and let him have his own way. The nurses were dismissed on Saturday, and he came down to tea. On Sunday evening, when Richard rang up as usual for news, Johnny was able to tell him that his great-uncle appeared to be perfectly well again.

Mercator joined them again for coffee the next morning and told them that he was expecting another guest for lunch. 'My solicitor — Christopher Sheringham. A very pleasant young man, and extremely good at his job. A highly creditable war record, too. You don't know him, I suppose, Heldar?'

'I've never met him, but I think he was up at Oxford

in my time — a year or two senior to me. Isn't he Dork-ing, Sheringham, and Dorking?'

'Yes. The original Sheringham was his great-grand-father. A good old family firm, like your own. They've acted for the Thaxtons for the last hundred years or so. My own solicitors took in new blood between the wars, and I didn't like it much, so I changed, and I've never had cause to regret it.'

Sally liked the look of Christopher Sheringham, though her mind compared him, as it did all men, un-favourably with Johnny. He was of middle height and well set up, fair, and good-looking in a pleasant, rather conventional way. He was a couple of years older than Johnny — thirty-six or thirty-seven, then. But where Johnny's profession would have been hard to guess, Sheringham had the stamp of the successful lawyer. He was not too smooth to be likeable, however, and he was excellent company. Lunch was, at first, a very easy and pleasant meal.

They were near the end of it when Richard arrived. He walked into the dining room unannounced and greeted Mercator quite cheerfully. He had gradually re-laxed last week as his great-uncle's condition had im-proved, and in the first moment of his arrival Sally thought he looked better and calmer than when he had left them. Then he stiffened suddenly, the old taut look came back to his face, and she saw that his eyes were on Christopher Sheringham. She saw, too, Sheringham's embarrassment. For a few seconds it was astonishingly plain.

Mercator was aware of the situation too, and she wondered if he could have explained it. He covered the difficult moment skilfully, welcoming Richard and bringing them all together into a family party. But the damage was done. Richard's nerves were raw again, and his eyes were bright with anger. He sat down and ate what Fenton brought him, talking in his brittle voice to Mercator and the Heldars, ignoring Sheringham, and yet unable to keep his eyes off him.

It was Deane who, in all innocence, brought the secret out. In a brief moment of silence he said with a gallant attempt at conversation: 'And how is Miss Harz?'

Richard said sharply: 'She's very well, thank you.' His eyes were on Sheringham again, and the naked jealousy in them was painful to see.

Sally, who was not as a rule very good at saving situations, made a desperate effort and got the conversation back to where it had been before.

It wasn't until twenty past two that the party broke up — for the moment, at any rate. Deane retired to his own room. Richard, who wanted a word with his great-uncle, was led off to Mercator's study, and Sheringham was left, with apologies, in the drawing room, until such time as Richard's business should be finished. Sally and Johnny escaped to the library.

'Well, that was an awkward scene,' said Johnny. 'I wonder how much there is behind it. I should say that Sheringham's intentions were entirely honourable; he's a decent, thoroughly conventional type, and if that wasn't enough, he's quite sufficiently shrewd to know that in a firm like his he couldn't afford even a minor scandal. I should think, if there's anything in it at all, he hoped to marry Lisa. He probably saw quite a lot of her over the proving of Richard's Will and the sale of the place.'

'There's something in it,' said Sally, 'or he wouldn't have looked so uncomfortable.'

'True. But Richard can't see straight at the moment. However honourable Sheringham's intentions were, he'd resent them bitterly.'

'She's extremely attractive,' said Sally slowly.

'Oh, tremendously,' said Johnny. But his voice was satisfactorily detached.

'She might throw even a respectable lawyer off his balance.'

Johnny looked at her thoughtfully. 'The *femme fatale?*' he asked. 'Yes, I think that's possible. In my experience — which hasn't been personal, Sally — the real *femme fatale* is generally a woman who hasn't the remotest idea of her own power. It's just that that makes her so dangerous. There was an ATS clerk during the war. She was quite an ordinary little girl — she'd been a typist, I think — and she wasn't unusually beautiful. She was entirely innocent — a little prudish, even — and rather stupid. But one man shot himself because of her; one perfectly good marriage broke up, and two of my own men became such useless soldiers that I had to have them transferred. It is possible that Lisa is that type. It's a poor look-out for Richard if she is.'

They worked steadily until a quarter to four, when they knocked off as usual for tea. They were not anxious to join the family party again, but it was possible that Richard, and perhaps Sheringham too, had left. As they reached the foot of the staircase, they saw Fenton approach the door of the study. He opened it and stood for a moment on the threshold. Then they heard him cry: 'Sir Mark!' and saw him plunge forward.

* * *

MERCATOR HAD FALLEN BACK in his chair, and his head had dropped forward. The attitude was natural enough — he might almost have been asleep — and yet there was something strangely final about it. Beside him, between the chair and the window, stood Colonel Danby, his brick-red face unpleasantly patched with white.

Johnny put the hovering butler aside and bent over

the still figure. He took Mercator's wrist in his fingers and held it for a moment. Then he said quietly: 'I'm afraid he's dead.'

'He got up too soon,' said Fenton shakily. 'He should have taken things easier.'

Johnny didn't answer at once. He was still bending down. He put his fingers under Mercator's chin, and gently raised his head. Then he said, still quietly: 'No, I don't think so. I'm afraid it wasn't a natural death.'

'What?' The Colonel was spluttering a little. 'Nonsense. He had a stroke, or after-effects of concussion. He was an old man.'

'Look there, sir.' Johnny seemed to be pointing at Mercator's Adam's apple. Danby peered at it.

'Dammit, boy, that's only a little bruise. It wouldn't kill anyone. Anyway, no one would hit him on the throat if they wanted to kill him. They'd hit him on the head. He must have knocked himself against something.'

'He wouldn't be likely to knock his throat, sir. That's a particularly vulnerable spot, you know, and I'm afraid someone may have gone for it deliberately.'

The Colonel roared suddenly: 'Are you accusing me of doing this, sir?'

'I'm very far from accusing anyone.' Johnny's voice was respectful, but firm. 'But I think we must have the police.'

'I'm a Justice of the Peace...' Danby's voice died away. He moved to one of the wing chairs and sat down heavily. 'All right. I suppose you're right. I'm too old for this sort of thing.'

'Sally,' said Johnny, 'go and fetch Richard and Sheringham, if they're still here, and Deane, and bring them to the hall.'

Sheringham was alone in the drawing room, sitting in one of the brocaded chairs, and apparently dozing over a magazine. He woke with a start, rose quickly, and said: 'Mrs Heldar — what is it?'

She told him, her words stumbling a little, and he said: 'Stay here,' and ran out of the room and along to the hall. Sally knocked on the door of Deane's room.

Deane seemed to have some difficulty in understanding what had happened. But at last she got him to the hall, where the Colonel and Fenton were waiting.

Then she went to the front door. A grey Morris stood in the courtyard, but Richard's Armstrong was gone.

* * *

THE VILLAGE CONSTABLE CAME FIRST, but nothing very much happened until a small body of police — plain clothes men and uniformed constables — arrived from Fanchester. The plain clothes men were closeted in the study, where they were presently joined by a man who seemed to be the police surgeon. He was followed almost at once by Dr Hill, who had been out in the country when Sheringham had telephoned for him. One of the constables remained in attendance on the little group in the hall. Presently two of the plain clothes men went along to the library. Then one of them came out again and went to Colonel Danby.

'Inspector Mason's compliments, sir, and he would be glad of a word with you.'

Danby puffed out his cheeks, said: 'Certainly...certainly,' in a voice which tried to be bluff and noticeably failed, and went off with the plain clothes man.

After that, the real waiting seemed to begin. The little group sat uneasily, scarcely speaking, for the presence of the constable seemed to make the most commonplace remark a matter of potential import. Sally, looking round, thought that, after Johnny, Christopher

Sheringham was the calmest of them. He sat quite still, and his face was expressionless. But his impassivity in itself suggested wariness and concealment. It was professional, of course. Deane, on the other hand, was patently nervous. Sometimes his bony fingers beat a tattoo on the arm of his chair. Sometimes a muscle twitched in his cheek, and though his eyes were restless they met no one else's. The Colonel, when he returned, was extremely uncomfortable. At intervals he blew out his cheeks and snorted a little, and now and then his hand went to his breast-pocket and then fell away again, as if he wanted to smoke, but kept remembering where he was. Johnny, steady as a rock, sat beside Sally on a high-backed sofa, and out of sight of the others his hand held hers in a firm, reassuring grip.

After the Colonel, Fenton was interviewed, and returned to sit on the edge of a chair with his eyes on the ground. Then it was Johnny's turn, and after that, Sally's.

Inspector Mason rose from his chair behind the big oak table, on which the catalogues and the Heldars' papers had been neatly stacked to one side. He was a ruddy-faced, stocky man, more like a farmer than a policeman, and he spoke in a slow Hampshire voice.

'Come in and sit down, Mrs Heldar. This is a very nasty business for you. And a sad one, perhaps.'

'We were very fond of Sir Mark,' said Sally gravely.

'That's what I thought, from the way Mr Heldar spoke of him. I never met him myself, but he was a very kind old gentleman from all accounts. Now, Mrs Heldar, I understand you arrived at the door of the study just after the butler. I'd like a full description of what you saw and what happened.'

When she had done her best with that Mason took her back to lunchtime. He wanted to know the time of Richard's arrival, which she thought had been a little after half-past one, and the time at which the party had broken up.

'It was just about twenty past two,' she said. 'I remember looking at the clock on the mantelpiece as we got up.'

'Very good. Now, where was everybody going at that time?'

'Mr Deane went to his room, next to the drawing room. Mr Sheringham stayed in the drawing room, and my husband and I came in here.'

'And Squadron Leader Thaxton went with Sir Mark to the study?'

'I believe so. We didn't actually see them go in.'

'Now what exactly was the arrangement, if we can call it that, made between Sir Mark and Squadron Leader Thaxton and Mr Sheringham? What did they say when the party broke up?'

'As far as I remember, Squadron Leader Thaxton said he would like to talk to Sir Mark. Sir Mark agreed and said they would go to his study. He asked Mr Sheringham to wait, and to make himself comfortable, and suggested he should go and have a look at the garden.'

'But Mr Sheringham didn't go out to the garden at once?'

'No. Not while we were still there.'

'Did Sir Mark give him any idea of how long he might be kept waiting? Or did Squadron Leader Thaxton?'

'Sir Mark said he was afraid they might be about half an hour, or perhaps longer, but he would come and fetch Mr Sheringham when they had finished.'

'His mention of a time-limit rather suggests that he either knew what Squadron Leader Thaxton wanted to talk to him about or had something he wanted to talk to Squadron Leader Thaxton about. Doesn't it? Have you any idea what either of those subjects could be?'

'No, I haven't. I assume they wanted to discuss a business or a family matter.'

'I'm sorry, Mrs Heldar. But I had to ask you that question. This may be murder, you know.' His blue eyes looked into hers, steady, solemn, and entirely honest.

Then he asked her several more questions. Between two-twenty and approximately three-forty-five, when she and Johnny had gone to the study, had either of them left the library? Had anyone else come into the library? Had she seen or heard anyone pass the open windows, or heard anyone pass the door? Had she heard any car? The answer to all these was no, but Sally explained that cataloguing was very concentrated work, and that she couldn't swear that no one had passed on the terrace, or that a car hadn't passed within earshot. The walls and doors were thick, and so were the carpets, and they might not have heard someone pass the door even if they had been listening.

Mason nodded, and then asked her suddenly about the quarrel between Mercator and Danby on her first evening at Westwater. She couldn't help smiling a little. But she didn't think Johnny would have volunteered this information. Probably Fenton had heard the Colonel's parade ground voice.

'It wasn't a very serious quarrel,' she said. 'It was really rather a joke — a good act. Sir Mark enjoyed it immensely. He wasn't really angry at all.' She stopped, and then wished she hadn't.

'But the Colonel was?'

'Only up to a point, I think. He enjoyed it in a way too. I rather think he's one of these men who thrive on rows.'

Mason smiled a little. 'Maybe. You say Sir Mark enjoyed it. Does that mean he didn't try to stop it — to calm the Colonel down?'

'Well, not at first. But as soon as—' She saw the little trap too late.

'As soon as what, Mrs Heldar?'

It would have to be the truth, she decided. 'As soon as it showed the faintest sign of getting out of hand, my husband intervened — quite gently — and they both calmed down at once.' She paused. 'It never struck me for one moment, Inspector, that the quarrel could be really serious, or could possibly lead to...to any serious consequences.'

Mason looked at her closely. 'Thank you, Mrs Heldar,' he said after a moment. 'I know that's an honest statement, and I appreciate it. Well, I think that's all for the moment. I'll get what you've told me typed out and ask you to go over it later on.'

Sheringham was interviewed, and then Deane, and after that the servants came. The maids had all been crying, and Emmanuel's eyes and Antoine's were red too. Even the stolid English chauffeur looked stricken. Sally remembered all the labour-saving gadgets in the east wing, and the pleasure in the servants' faces when Mercator wandered in upon them.

* * *

AFTER A LONG TIME Mason came back to the hall. He stood before them solid and four-square, and said quietly: 'I'm sorry to have had to keep you here so long. You're free now to move about as you wish, but I must ask you not to leave the grounds until further notice. Except for you, sir.' He nodded to the Colonel. 'I expect you'll want to get home. And might I just have another word with you, Mr Deane?'

Cecil Deane turned paler than before, stumbled to his feet, and followed the Inspector. The rest of the group avoided each other's eyes for a moment. Then the Colonel heaved himself up and said: 'Well, I'd better be off. If you should want me, let me know. Anything I can do for young Richard. The police are getting in touch with him. Most unfortunate he should have left when he did — must have been only a short time before we found — er — his uncle.' He stopped short, and a look of horrified discomfort came into his face.

'That's very good of you, sir,' said Sheringham calmly. 'I'll tell him you're ready to help.' He escorted Danby to the door.

Sally said suddenly: 'How does he know when Richard left? None of us do, do we?'

'Possibly Fenton,' said Johnny. 'But I don't think so. Perhaps Danby met Richard.' He took Sally's arm. 'Let's go upstairs for a little while. I expect Sheringham will excuse us.'

They went up to their room and sat on the window seat. The garden and the trees of the park lay quiet in the late sunlight. On the west avenue the Colonel appeared, walking slowly towards a car which was parked a short distance from the house. They watched him get into it, turn it rather clumsily, and drive away down the avenue.

'This doesn't mean that Mason's ruled him out, I suppose?' asked Sally.

'No. I don't see how Mason can rule anyone out at this stage. But it would be difficult not to let Danby go home when he lives so near.'

'We never heard him arrive. Mason asked me if I'd heard a car.'

They compared notes and found that Mason had asked them almost exactly the same questions and received almost exactly the same answers. But there was one thing which had been worrying Sally, and apparently Johnny too.

'I didn't tell Mason,' he said, 'about Willesdon

coming here the evening we arrived. I'm not sure that I was right, but there's absolutely nothing to suggest that he was here this afternoon. All the same, we may have to report it. It depends—'

They were interrupted at that point by Annie. She smiled at them a little tremulously, but her voice was calm.

'Supper will be ready in about twenty minutes, madam. I'm afraid it'll only be cold beef and salad; Mr Ongtoyne's very upset, and he can't cook when he's upset; he's French, you understand, madam. But Fenton's taking drinks to the drawing room. You're looking very tired, madam; you'd be the better of a glass of sherry.'

But they were intercepted on their way to the drawing room. Mason was in the hall, and he wanted to talk to them again.

When they were sitting round the library table he said unexpectedly: 'You and Mrs Heldar are experts on books. Do you know a book called *Garland for Gloriana*, by Sir Harry Percival?'

'Yes,' said Johnny. 'It was first published in 1588, and it's a book of rather charming poems dedicated by the author to Elizabeth I.'

'Was there a copy of it in this library?'

'There was.' Johnny paused. 'But it seems to have disappeared under rather curious circumstances. I didn't mention it before, because it never struck me that it could be relevant to Sir Mark's death. But you can judge that better than I can.'

He told the story of the apparent substitution, explaining the technical points clearly and simply, but without talking down to the Inspector, and illustrating the explanation with the title page of the reprint, which Mason produced from a drawer. Mason listened attentively, and then asked him directly if they had suspected anyone. Johnny admitted it reluctantly, and explained the difficulties involved in the disposal of rare books as stolen property, and his reasons for thinking that Richard might have got away with it. He was rather formal and a little terse; he wasn't enjoying this.

When he had finished Mason sat for a moment looking down at the reprint. Then he seemed to make up his mind. He opened a drawer and took out a sheet of letter-paper. 'As a bookseller and an expert, Mr Heldar, what do you make of that?'

Sally leaned over to read it. The letter was neatly typed below the printed Westwater letterhead.

11th August 1954

JAMES MUMFORD, ESQ,
18B FINMARK STREET,
LONDON, WC1

DEAR MR MUMFORD,

On the 28th of July last, the bearer, who is my private secretary, sold to you on my instructions a copy of the First (1588) Edition of Percival's Garland for Gloriana, and received for it the fair price of ninety-five pounds. On my instructions, again, he did not disclose the facts that he was acting on my behalf, and that the book formed part of the Thaxton Library, which I had purchased from the heir of the apparently late Squadron Leader Richard Thaxton.

As you may have learnt from your daily newspaper, Squadron Leader Thaxton has now returned to life. It is therefore eminently desirable that the volume in question be restored to his library as soon as possible. If it has not yet passed out of your hands, I shall be glad to repurchase it for the sum of one hundred and twenty pounds, for which amount I enclose my cheque. If it has already been sold, I shall be most grateful if you will supply the name and address of the purchaser.

Yours sincerely,

The letter was unsigned.

'Do you know the firm, to start with?' asked Mason.

'Oh, yes,' said Johnny. 'Very well. Harold Mumford and Son. They're old-established and entirely honest and respectable.'

'Mr Heldar, you knew Sir Mark and you know the ways of book-collectors, which I don't. Would he have been likely to sell that book?'

After a moment Johnny said: 'No. It was a rare book and an interesting one, and it was part of a valuable and interesting library which he would never have wanted to break up and which was in a sense family property. And even if he had decided to sell it, he would never have done it in that underhand way — concealing from the book world that he was selling the Thaxton copy — and he would never in this world have substituted the reprint. That would be dead against collector's morals, which aren't always quite the same as the average man's morals, but which form a very strong code for all that. I admit that his manner when we told him about the substitution was consistent with his having done it himself, but it's quite impossible that he should have done.'

Mason nodded. 'Do you agree, Mrs Heldar?'

'Oh, yes,' said Sally. 'It's out of the question.'

'I see. And of course the question of money would never arise. Now, Mr Heldar. Acting on Sir Mark's instructions or not, do you think Mr Deane could have sold that book to Mr Mumford without inviting awkward questions?'

'I think he probably could,' said Johnny. 'He's a very nervous type, and not, I should think, a good actor, and I doubt very much if he'd have got past the average antiquarian bookseller. But Mumford is rather an unusual proposition. His knowledge is enormous, but since this is a police enquiry I'd better admit that he's a far better connoisseur than he is a business man. He's a little vague and rather unworldly, and the firm hasn't really prospered since his father died. It gets along, you know, and he's perfectly happy, but that's about all.'

'And would Sir Mark have been likely to know Mr Mumford's character?'

'I should think so. Sir Mark had been frequenting the antiquarian booksellers of London for about fifty years.'

'Just so. Have you yourself had correspondence with Sir Mark?'

'Yes, often,' said Johnny. 'This letter is very much in his style. If I'd received it, I'd have seen no reason to suspect it.'

'Well, thank you very much, Mr Heldar. And Mrs Heldar. There's only one more question I wanted to ask you. Did you ever hear Sir Mark mention anyone called Klaus? Like Santa Claus, only spelt with a K instead of a C. I don't quite know if I'm pronouncing it right.'

'I've never heard him mention the name,' said Johnny, and Sally shook her head. 'It's a German name, and I know he had business relations with Germany, but that's all I can suggest, I'm afraid.'

* * *

SHERINGHAM STOOD up as they came into the drawing room.

'A distinctly difficult afternoon,' he said. 'No one of us is host to the others, but since Fenton has been kind enough to provide drinks, please allow me to get you some.'

He brought Sally a sherry, and Johnny a gin and tonic, and sat down again with his own glass in his

dinary punch, which he didn't manage to take on the chin.'

'Then it might have been anyone.'

Johnny nodded.

'Could Richard have learnt that blow in his prison camp? Judo is Japanese, isn't it?'

'Yes. It might have been known in a Chinese POW camp.'

'Then if it was deliberate—?'

'No one else is very likely to have known the blow. Christopher was a gunner. Deane was too young for the war, and obviously doesn't go in for physical exercise of any kind. Danby may conceivably have learnt Judo in his day, but I doubt it. I'm not much impressed by Danby as a suspect, anyway. Perhaps it's largely due to reading detective stories — the man who is found bending over the body with a smoking revolver in his hand is *never* the murderer. But Danby is an Army man, and however hot-tempered a regular Army man may be, he generally has an underlying discipline which prevents him from doing violence.' Johnny stopped. 'I'm sorry, darling. You like Richard, don't you?'

'Yes. But if he killed Mercator — deliberately—'

She remembered the servants' faces, and the portrait in the study, where Mercator had died. She hadn't wanted to cry till now.

CHAPTER FOUR

They lay awake for some time that night and were sleeping heavily when Annie brought up their breakfast and some letters which their daily had forwarded from the flat. News from the outside world seemed rather remote and unreal. There was a picture postcard of Penzance from young Tim Heldar, a couple of bills for Johnny, and a note for Sally from Elizabeth Rawlings, who had failed to get her on the telephone and wanted them to come to dinner tonight. Elizabeth would have to be rung up. So, said Johnny, would his grandfather, who had been a friend of Mercator's for fifty years. They were on the point of going downstairs to do it when Christopher knocked on the dressing room door. His neat town clothes seemed faintly out of place this morning, and he looked a little jaded.

'I'm so sorry to disturb you,' he said, 'but there's a question I'd like to put to you — as Mercator's solicitor. Did he ask you to witness a will for him? Or did he say anything which suggested that he was going to make one?'

Sally shook her head, and Johnny said: 'No. He said nothing whatever about a will.'

'Thank you. By the way, I suppose you haven't seen Deane this morning?'

'We haven't; no.'

Christopher hesitated a moment. Then he said: 'I'm a little anxious about him. He's not in the house. It seems that Emmanuel took up his breakfast just before half-past eight, and he wasn't there. His bed had been slept in all right, but Emmanuel looked everywhere and couldn't find him. He may be in the grounds, of course, but it's after half-past nine, and I think we ought to make sure.'

'I agree,' said Johnny. 'Would you like to come, Sally, or stay here?'

'I'll come,' said Sally.

But as they came to the gallery, they heard voices in the hall. Dr Hill's voice, and Mason's.

'I'm sorry, Inspector,' Hill was saying, 'but he is not fit to be questioned. You must have seen that for yourself last night. He's in an abnormal nervous condition at the moment, and when you consider what he's been through, it's not surprising.'

'All right, Doctor,' said Mason slowly. 'I won't press the point now. But I think I must ask for a second opinion.'

'Very well. If Dr Palliser says he's fit, that's fair enough, but I won't be answerable for the consequences. I think Palliser will agree with me, though.'

Christopher had said quietly to Johnny: 'Better carry on if I'm detained,' and walked down the staircase.

'Good morning, Inspector,' he said. 'As Squadron Leader Thaxton's solicitor, can I be of any use to you?'

Mason smiled — a slow, faintly amused smile. 'Perhaps we might try, Mr Sheringham. May we go into the library?'

Johnny led Sally down to the hall and greeted the

doctor and the constable on duty there. Then he moved unhurriedly on to the drawing room, and out on to the terrace.

The grounds, as opposed to the park, were not very large. But the couple of acres on the south side, with the formal garden, the kitchen garden, the stables, and various shrubberies, were not easy to search in a hurry, and Johnny wouldn't let Sally leave him. 'We've got to be quick, though,' he said. 'I don't really like this copper's nark act, but Christopher would be in an awkward position if he had to admit that he suspected Deane was gone and let Mason go without telling him.'

They ran into the gardener's boy, and met the chauffeur in the stable-yard, and Johnny asked them, casually, if they had seen Mr Deane. They hadn't. But a few minutes later the Heldars found the under-gardener picking peas, and at Johnny's question he showed signs of embarrassment. Johnny ceased to be casual. It was fairly clear that the young man had been in the Army, for he recognised Johnny's manner, and almost at once the truth came out.

'Yes, sir, I did see 'im; 'e got on the early bus about 'alf-way along the park wall from the village. I was takin' the short cut through the park to my work, an' I saw 'im get over the wall an' signal to the driver, an' the bus stopped for 'im.'

'What time was that?'

'It would be just after a quarter to eight, sir. The bus leaves the village at a quarter to eight.'

'And it goes where?'

'Fanchester, sir.'

'I see. What's your name? Betts, isn't it? Right.'

The Heldars came out of the drawing room just as Christopher and Mason were leaving the library. Christopher, cautious as ever, gave them no lead. But Johnny said quietly: 'I'm afraid Deane has gone.'

'What's that?' said Mason.

Christopher and Johnny told him. He received their news calmly and seemed to accept their motive for looking first and telling him afterwards. Then he retired into the telephone room. That reminded the Heldars of their own telephoning, and they waited till he came out.

Johnny told his grandfather gently but directly about Mercator's death. He gave no details, for he didn't trust the discretion of the local exchange. As he had expected, the news hadn't been in the morning's papers, though the later editions would certainly make a meal of it, and he had wanted to get in before them. But Old Father William Heldar had taken a good many blows in his long life, and he took this one quite quietly.

'Now Elizabeth,' said Johnny. 'Better just tell her we're out of town on a job, darling. Say Hampshire if necessary, but don't go into details.'

Sally nodded. She couldn't remember Elizabeth's number, and she opened the L to R volume of the Directory. She saw something lying between the pages — something which looked like the edge of a sheet of thick paper — and opened the volume again at that point to see what it was.

It was a foolscap envelope inscribed in a large, rather shaky and hesitant hand.

The Last Will and Testament of
MARK JONATHAN MERCATOR
of Mercator House, London, EC2

To my Executors:
JACOB DAVID RATHBONE,
of Mercator House, London, EC2
and
CHRISTOPHER WINFORD SHERINGHAM,

of New Square, London, WC2

She had cried out, and Johnny was reading the inscription over her shoulder.

'Well, I'll be damned,' he said. 'This would appear to be the will that Christopher is so interested in. Though why it should have been put here is beyond me. We'd better hand it over to him.' He took the envelope and slid it into his inside breast-pocket.

The constable was still on duty in the hall, but Johnny gave Christopher a cheerful smile and the flicker of an eyebrow and strolled out of the front door with Sally. When they came round the end of the west wing Christopher was strolling towards them.

'Well?' he asked.

Johnny produced the envelope. 'My wife found this,' he said, 'in the L to R volume of the London Telephone Directory. You would appear to be the correct recipient.' Then he led Sally off across the lawn.

* * *

A LITTLE LATER, when Mason had questioned them closely about the finding of the will, and Sally had at last put through her call to Elizabeth, Lisa joined the Heldars in the drawing room. She was wearing a little black summer suit, and she looked paler than ever, and still very tired. Johnny got up and gave her a cigarette, and Sally asked her how Richard was.

'He is not well,' she said wearily. 'He has had a bad night, and I knew this morning that he was not fit to be questioned again. That is why I sent for Dr Hill. I was afraid he might not stand by us, but he did. The police doctor will probably say that Richard is fit. But Mason has gone for the moment, so at least we have gained a little time, and that is what I want to talk to you about. I have come to ask your help — for Richard.'

'What do you want us to do?' asked Johnny.

Lisa looked earnestly at him. 'I want that everyone who was here yesterday afternoon shall say openly to everyone else what they were doing, where they were, what they saw, and what they heard. Also what they have said to the police about it. Not the servants, for I think they were all about their business in the east wing. It may be necessary to question Fenton, but probably none of the others. And Deane is gone — that may mean he is guilty, of course, but we cannot be sure. But if everyone else will help, some information, some evidence favourable to Richard may appear, and at least he will know where he stands, and what he must contend with. Will you please help him in this way? It cannot hurt you, for you can be in no danger. You had, I suppose, an opportunity of killing Sir Mark — as everyone else had — but you could have had no possible reason for doing so. I have telephoned to Colonel Danby, and he is willing — he is coming over now.'

Johnny said slowly: 'What does Sheringham say to this, Lisa? After all, he's Richard's solicitor, and he may be the best person to help him.'

She shook her head. 'No,' she said, quietly and definitely. 'Christopher can't help Richard — except perhaps with his own evidence. He is a bad psychologist. Besides' — she hesitated — 'he and Richard are not on good terms just now. He doesn't know how to deal with Richard in his present condition, and Richard is not well enough to overcome his irritation with him. He tried to talk to Richard this morning, before Dr Hill came, and it was useless. Richard simply became angry and could not talk reasonably. He answered a few of Christopher's questions — about this will and so on — but that was all. I tried to calm him, but it was no good.

So I am suggesting this other way. Christopher does not approve, of course, but I believe he is wrong.'

Sally couldn't help wondering whether, if Richard was unfit to talk to his solicitor, he was really fit for a full-scale council of war. But that wasn't her business, and Lisa was quite likely to be right. Evidently Johnny thought so too, for he said: 'All right. We'll help.'

'Thank you,' said Lisa gently. 'I am very grateful.' Then she tilted her head a little, listening. 'I think that must be Colonel Danby.'

They heard the car stop, with a squealing of brakes, and a minute or two later Danby appeared at the window. Sally, understanding from Lisa's faint hesitation that she had met him only on the telephone, made introductions, and the Colonel became at the same time gallant and paternal.

'So you're Richard's fiancée. Well, I think he's a very lucky man. I don't know exactly what you want me to do, but I'll help you both in any way I can. I was an old friend of Richard's father, you know, and I've seen the boy grow up.'

He told Lisa her idea was an excellent one. It was perfectly clear than any idea of Lisa's would have seemed excellent to him, but he was certainly a whole-hearted ally. 'And if anything helpful crops up, I can bring it to the notice of the police. Matter of fact, I was just thinking of going and having a palaver with the Chief Constable when you rang up.'

Lisa thanked him, and then led them all to the staircase in the west wing. She said, quite truthfully as it turned out, that it was the quickest way to Richard's room, but Sally suspected that she was more concerned with avoiding the constable in the hall.

Mercator hadn't shown the Heldars Richard's room, which was in the nineteenth-century building, and he had obviously left it untouched. The bars at the windows suggested that it had originally been a nursery. Now it was the room of a schoolboy and of a very young man — Richard hadn't been much at Westwater since he had grown up — but a young man with some subtlety of taste. The Victorian furniture was plain and rather battered. The faded floral wallpaper was hung with school groups, a good print of Paul Nash's *Battle of Britain,* and some reproductions of da Vinci's sketches. Two silver trophies and a model aircraft stood on the broad mantelpiece. The bookshelves contained a mixture of boys' books and post-war poetry.

But Sally took in these details only gradually. She was more interested in Richard himself. He had dressed, and was wearing old slacks and a sports shirt, with a silk scarf tucked into it instead of a tie. But he was looking very ill indeed. Christopher, who was with him, looked dignified and disapproving.

Someone had evidently brought in some extra chairs, and Richard asked them all to sit down. Then he said in a carefully controlled voice — forestalling the Colonel, who had been on the point of taking charge of the proceedings: 'I think Lisa has told you what we're asking you to do. We shall both be extremely grateful if you'll help. I'm going to take the first turn and tell you exactly what happened between my uncle and me yesterday afternoon. If anyone has any comment to make, please stop me and make it.'

'One minute, Richard,' said Christopher. 'I think I must make it clear that no one is under any obligation to make any sort of statement at all. Anyone who makes one makes it of his own free will and on his own responsibility.'

Richard sat very still and said nothing. The Colonel said irritably: 'Yes, yes, of course, Sheringham. We all know that.'

Richard went on. 'I came down yesterday to discuss

with my uncle the question of my engagement to Lisa. Lisa herself has agreed that I explain to you just why it had to be discussed. My uncle had an unreasonable prejudice against Germans. One can't altogether blame him; he was Jewish, and his only daughter and most of his other relatives died in Nazi concentration camps. But he always tried very hard to overcome his dislike — I think it worried him a bit, because in most things he was a very just man — and I didn't anticipate any serious trouble over Lisa. He was abroad when we got engaged, and I went to Korea straight after that without seeing him. I had a general impression, from his letters and Lisa's, that he wasn't very enthusiastic, and then, of course, I heard no more for years. When I got back, I hoped to be able to sort things out. But on the first afternoon we were down here — the day of his accident — he took me along to the study and asked me quite quietly to reconsider my engagement. I asked him why, and he was cagey. I suggested it was merely because Lisa was German, and he didn't deny it. He seemed very unhappy about it, and I ought to have talked it over quietly, but I lost my temper. I walked out on him, collected Lisa, and drove back to town.

'After his accident we got back on better terms, but the matter wasn't mentioned again before Lisa and I left on Friday. But I knew we'd have to have it out when he was better. I wouldn't have come back so soon, but Lisa was very distressed by his attitude, and trying to break off our engagement. I was going to be very quiet and reasonable with Mark yesterday and try and talk him round. But it didn't work out that way.

'When we went along to the study, we talked a bit of business first. Then he raised the question of my engagement himself, and suddenly pulled a punch that took my breath away. I ought to explain that up to the time I was shot down I was his heir. He never made any secret of it; I'd known it for years. When he thought I was dead he naturally made a new will, and by that he left most of his money to various suitable charities. Yesterday he took a sheet of paper from his desk and told me that this was his latest will and by it he left everything to me, on condition that I didn't marry Lisa. At least, his money was left in trust, and the income would be paid to me as long as I fulfilled the condition. If I married Lisa at any time, the income would go to charity.

'That finished me, I'm afraid. I didn't mind so very much about the money, though I didn't particularly want to lose twenty-five thousand a year. When things are settled up, I shall have quite enough for Lisa and myself. It was the injustice of it that got me, and the suggestion that I'd give up Lisa sooner than forfeit the money. So I lost my temper again. I said he could bloody well leave his money how he liked and walked out. I walked out by the study door and the front door and got into the car and drove away. That was just about a quarter to three. Somewhere beyond Guildford I began to cool off a bit, and my nerves came back at me.' He spoke harshly, and Sally knew that he hated his condition with the bitter shame of a man who was not habitually neurotic. 'I turned off the road and smoked some cigarettes — I don't know how long I was there, but I should think nearly an hour. Then I drove on to town rather slowly and went straight to Lisa's flat. I got there about a quarter to six, and about six o'clock a bobby turned up to break the news.

'When we got back here, I told Mason exactly what I've told you. He obviously hadn't found the will and was half inclined to think I was making it up. That question is now disposed of, but the disappearance and reappearance of the will is still a complete mystery. I may as well tell you that it was a homemade will, but drawn up in due form, dated the sixth of August — two days after his accident — and witnessed by his two nurses.

'Mason's second point of suspicion was my time of departure. He obviously didn't believe me when I said I'd left at a quarter to three. Nor did he believe me when I said I'd left by the north avenue, which is the normal one when you're going to London. He pressed me fairly hard, and then he said: "Supposing I told you that you had been seen just outside the west gate at twenty-five past three, going north?" I'd had just about enough by then, and I said: "I'd say you were trying to trap me." It was unforgivable, of course. And then I passed out. Mason brought me round, and then appeared to decide that that was enough for that evening. But I realise now that he's not a Chinese torturer, and he must have had some evidence for what he said.' He looked suddenly at the Colonel. 'What is it, sir?'

Danby was looking acutely uncomfortable. 'But Richard, my dear boy,' he said, 'you did leave by the west gate. It was I who saw you outside it — or at least I saw your car — and it was just about twenty-five past three. I told Mason. You must have forgotten.'

Richard said very quietly: 'I suppose that is possible. And if I've forgotten that—' His hands were gripping the arms of his chair.

'Wait,' said Johnny calmly. 'How did you know it was Richard's car, sir?'

'I've known it for years. Besides, it has a distinctive number.'

'Forgive me, sir, but you can't have known the car Richard was driving yesterday. Not for years, anyhow. It's a last year's Armstrong Siddeley Sapphire — the one he's brought down every time since he got back. I saw it through the open front door when we went along to the drawing room after lunch.'

'Yes,' said Richard sharply. 'That's Lisa's car.'

The Colonel was staring at Johnny. 'The car I saw,' he said, 'was Richard's old Rover, which he bought in...in...'

'Nineteen-forty-six,' said Richard.

'The number is QXQ 333. Anyhow, this is what happened. I heard from Mellis — my gardener — that you were down again. He'd seen some chap in the village who'd seen you arrive — he didn't say what car you were driving. I thought, as your uncle was better, I'd come and see you. I drove round to the west gate — nearest way for me — and when I came round the bend short of the gate I saw the Rover ahead. I assumed you were in it, and you'd just come out. I blew my horn, but you took no notice. I knew I couldn't catch you — the Rover was moving fast — so I let you go.'

'I see,' said Richard. 'Of course, if it had been me it would fit in well enough with the time I got back to town — if I hadn't been delayed *en route.*'

There was a short silence. Then Lisa said: 'Darling, it's no use. We must tell the truth about the Rover.'

'Yes, I suppose so,' said Richard abruptly. 'Well, when I went overseas, I left the Rover with Lisa. She was in a mews flat then and had a lock-up going begging. But the Rover isn't really a woman's car; it was pretty battered even then and needed a certain amount of attention to keep it going. So I told her that if she got sick of it she could turn it over to a friend of mine: an ex-RAF type called George Willesdon. He was out of a job and a bit down on his luck. But I was a fool to do it because he's a born scrounger. At first he didn't use the Rover much, but he had it when he wanted it and Lisa garaged it. Then, when my father was killed, he persuaded her to write to me and ask me to give him the job of land-agent here — my father's man was retiring. I was fool enough to agree, and as long as he was at

Westwater he had an estate car and didn't need the Rover. But when Mark bought the place, he sacked George for incompetence — quite rightly, I'm afraid, from what I've heard. Soon after that George came to Lisa — who had just bought the Armstrong and was thinking of selling the Rover — and said he'd been offered a job as a traveller in stationery and couldn't take it unless he had a car. So Lisa, in the kindness of her heart, said the Rover was his. But he continued to garage it free of charge under her flat. She could very easily have told him to take it away when she moved, which she did not long after. But she arranged for the new tenant of her flat to let her keep on the lock-up. George has gone through several jobs since then, and most of them have involved travelling. So the Rover is still his.'

There was another silence. Then Johnny said: 'I'm afraid Sally and I have something to add to this. We haven't told the police about it yet. But I think they'll have to know now.'

The story of Willesdon's visit to Mercator created a strong impression. Christopher looked keenly interested. Danby said: 'By Jove, he's our man! He was always a bad type — drunk and disorderly, and hopelessly incompetent. He came down again — perhaps he hoped to see Richard — quarrelled with Mercator and killed him.'

'We'll want a bit more evidence, sir,' said Richard unhappily. 'He'd have no motive for premeditated murder — I mean, he couldn't be at all sure that if Mark died he'd get his job back. Even if Mark hadn't had time to persuade me that he'd made a mess of things, Christopher knew all about it. Christopher found out all about it when he was settling up the estate, and George was only kept on until the place was sold because Lisa hadn't the heart to sack him.'

Johnny explained, reluctantly, that the murder hadn't necessarily been premeditated. Richard frowned, and said: 'All right. But why would George want to see Mark at all? There wouldn't be much point in trying to persuade Mark not to tell me about his shortcomings, when Christopher certainly would if Mark didn't. I was the man he wanted to see about it. He'd been ringing up Lisa's flat for the last few days, and Lisa had been putting him off.'

Lisa said wretchedly: 'That is true. But — he knew you were down here yesterday, Richard. He rang up just after you had left, and I told him you had gone to Westwater.'

'There you are,' said Danby. 'He came down thinking he'd corner you here, arrived after you'd left, and walked in on Mercator.'

There was yet another silence. Then Lisa said: 'We must go on. Will you go on, Colonel Danby? After you had let the Rover go?'

The Colonel looked a little disconcerted. 'Well, after that,' he said, 'I thought I'd have a look at Mercator's farm. You know we — er — we had a bit of a row about that. Well, fact is, I — er — I wanted to see if the work was still at a standstill, or if he'd persuaded you to let him carry on with it. I didn't drive back and up the lane; I left the car on the west avenue and walked across the park; it's only a few minutes. It looked to me as if some more work had been done, so I came back to the car and drove up to the house — to — er — find out from your uncle what was what, you know. I found him dead in his chair, and the next minute Fenton came in.'

Richard said gently: 'He hadn't gone on with the work, sir.'

The Colonel looked for a moment like an elderly baby about to burst into tears. Then he said: 'Well, anyway, there's no evidence that I went to the farm. I didn't

71

meet anyone. There's no evidence, I suppose, that I didn't come straight up to the house.'

Richard looked round. 'Did anyone hear the Colonel's car?'

It appeared that no one had heard any car between two-twenty and three-forty-five, and the meeting passed on to Christopher's evidence, which was skilfully extracted, under difficulties, by Lisa. After being left alone in the drawing room at two-twenty, he had gone out by the window and walked in the garden. He had met one of the gardeners at about two-thirty but had seen no one else. He had returned to the drawing room at two-forty-five, in order to be ready for Mercator, sat down with a magazine, and presently dozed off. He hadn't wakened until Sally had come to tell him that Mercator was dead.

Finally the Heldars made their statement. It was fairly short and simple and didn't help at all.

* * *

THERE WAS a general pause for thought, and in the middle of it a discreet knock fell on the door. Richard called: 'Come in!'

Fenton came in. A faint shade of anxiety seemed to lie over his face.

'Yes, Fenton?' asked Richard.

'If you will excuse me, Mr Richard.' He glanced almost imperceptibly round the little circle, as if he were not quite sure which of them was the proper recipient of his information. Then, perhaps, Richard's air of authority decided him.

'I felt it to be my duty to inform you, Mr Richard, that Gloria — that is, the parlourmaid — is in possession of certain information which may conceivably have a bearing, however indirect, upon Sir Mark's death.'

Richard's lips twitched very slightly. He said gravely: 'What information, Fenton?'

But Fenton was going to tell his story in his own way. 'The girl should undoubtedly have spoken before, Mr Richard. As I have told her, it was her duty to lay this information before Inspector Mason when he questioned her yesterday. She was, however, reluctant to incriminate a person who, she said, had shown her some kindness, and I think it fair to say, Mr Richard, that she was not fully aware of the potential significance of what she had observed.'

Richard smiled. 'Mr Sheringham will defend her from the wrath of Inspector Mason. Now, who is this person?'

'The girl, Mr Richard, was somewhat troubled in her conscience when she learned that Mr Deane was absent this morning and became more so when it was understood that he had — er — left the neighbourhood. She at last confided her doubts in Annie, who thought it proper to report the matter to me.'

'Quite right, Fenton. You'd better bring Gloria up.'

Fenton retired, and Christopher said: 'I think it might be better, Richard, if you and I questioned the girl alone.'

'No,' said Richard. 'We agreed on a pooling of information. We'll all see her.' He grinned suddenly. 'I do love Fenton's sentences, don't you? He never puts a word wrong.'

Gloria must have been left somewhere handy, for Fenton produced her almost at once, and retired again himself. She was very young — Sally had already put her down as a country girl being trained under the butler — and very small and shy. She stood just inside the door, making a desperate effort to keep her hands from twisting her apron, and she had obviously been crying.

Christopher cleared his throat, but Richard silenced him with a gesture and got up. 'You're Gloria Worsley,' he said.

'Yes, sir.' It was a barely audible whisper.

'Old William Worsley must be your grandfather.'

'That's right, sir.'

Richard laughed. 'He's a great friend of mine. He used to take me out fishing when I was a boy. Not always by daylight, either.'

Gloria smiled. ''E told me about that, Mr Richard.' Her careful parlourmaid's English was beginning to slip, laying bare the natural Hampshire underneath. She had come forward now and was standing before Richard.

'The old villain,' said Richard. 'Tell him I'll be over to see him. Well, Gloria, you've got something you feel you must tell us about Mr Deane. You didn't want to tell it because he was kind to you?'

'No, Mr Richard.' She looked earnestly up at him as he towered over her, and Sally realised suddenly that with his astounding smile and his painful record he was probably the personification of the heroes of all the women's-magazine stories she had ever read. The tears came into her eyes again, and Sally thought that they weren't only for Deane.

''E was always kind to me,' she said. 'I don't mean Sir Mark wasn't; Sir Mark was the kindest gentleman I ever knew. But I felt sort of lost when I first came — it's a big 'ouse when you're not used to it — an' Mr Deane was kind to me too. I don't mean nothin' wrong, Mr Richard; 'e was always a gentleman. But just a nice friendly word when 'e saw me. I used to think p'r'aps 'e felt a bit lost too.'

'That's quite possible,' said Richard. 'Well, what happened, Gloria?'

'Well, Mr Richard, I was cleanin' the silver yesterday afternoon, an' I was goin' into the dinin' room to put some of it away. It was just five past three. I came out of the green baize door, an' I saw Mr Deane just goin' into the study. 'E didn't see me.'

There was a startled silence. Then Richard said: 'You didn't see him come out again?'

'No, Mr Richard. There wasn't no sign of 'im when I came out of the dinin' room.'

'You are quite sure it was five past three, Gloria?'

'Yes, Mr Richard, an' Mr Fenton'll say the same. 'E came in while I was cleanin' the silver, an' 'e looked at the pantry clock an' said I'd 'ave to 'urry if I was to finish it before tea time.'

Fenton, recalled, confirmed the point. Richard asked him tactfully for an account of his movements on the previous afternoon, and discovered that after about two-thirty, when he had removed the coffee tray from the drawing room — and when, incidentally, Christopher had not been there — he hadn't left the east wing. Not until a quarter to four, when he had gone to the study to find out if, in view of Mercator's conference with Christopher, he should serve tea as usual at four. Between two-twenty and three-forty-five he had heard no car, and he believed himself to be safe in saying that none of the other servants had heard one either. From the east wing one could not hear a car on the west avenue. Under certain circumstances one could hear a car entering or leaving the courtyard, but from about twenty to three onwards he himself, Emmanuel, and Antoine had been for most of the time in the housekeeper's room, which was now their sitting room, and the maids — with the exception of Gloria — in the servants' hall. Both these rooms and the butler's pantry, where Gloria had been working, were on the east side, facing the kitchen court, and in the sitting room and the hall the wireless had been on, so it was extremely unlikely that any car would have been heard. It was also perfectly clear that, probably as a result of Mason's interrogation, this question had been exhaustively discussed in the east wing, and when Fenton and Gloria had withdrawn the meeting agreed that it was unnecessary to question the other servants.

It also agreed that certain information must be communicated to the police at once: the story of Willesdon and the Rover; the fact that Richard had been driving the Armstrong; Willesdon's quarrel with Mercator, and Gloria's evidence. The Colonel had fallen upon Gloria's evidence as indisputable proof, combined with his disappearance, of Deane's guilt. But Richard pointed out that, if Deane were guilty, the presence of the Rover had still to be explained. The Colonel grunted, agreed, and then announced his intention of reporting in person to the Chief Constable. It took the combined effort of everyone else to persuade him that it would be impolitic to by-pass Mason, and wiser to report in the first instance to the constable downstairs. There was also an unspoken feeling that Christopher would make a better spokesman than Danby, but finally a compromise was reached, and the two went downstairs together.

The Heldars were in their room when the gong sounded for lunch. As they came out into the corridor Lisa and Richard appeared from the direction of the west wing.

Lisa said a little anxiously: 'The police surgeon has been here. He would not commit himself to Richard or Christopher, one way or the other. I am afraid he will say Richard is fit to be questioned. But now Richard insists on coming down to lunch, and I do not think it is wise, with the policeman in the hall.'

Johnny glanced at Richard and said: 'Coming down to lunch in one's own home isn't quite the same as being questioned by the police.'

'It can't make much difference now, anyway,' said Richard. 'Palliser's seen me. And in any case, I'm going to see Mason this afternoon. When he heard our report from the constable, he said he'd come out.'

Lisa opened her mouth to protest, and then shut it again. She was staring at something over Sally's shoulder, and the others turned to follow her gaze. From where they stood they could see a section of the two galleries and look straight down the corridor opposite to theirs. Along it Deane was coming, stooped, angular, pale-faced, walking quietly and openly, as if he had never been out of the house.

CHAPTER FIVE

L unch was a strange meal — strange, because on the surface it was almost normal. Richard Thaxton sat at the head of his own table, under the portrait of Mercator's wife, whose features were extraordinarily like his own. But though his nerves were still taut, it wasn't this new position which troubled him; he might have held it for the last ten years. Sally sat on his right, and Lisa on his left, and although no one talked a great deal the conversation moved along. It was extremely hard to believe that the little scene in the hall had been real. Deane walking downstairs and into the constable's arms. The constable's questions, and Deane saying with fairly creditable calm that he had spent the morning walking in the park. No, he hadn't understood that the park was out of bounds. The constable asking him to remain in the hall, and disappearing into the telephone room, leaving the door open. Deane sitting down and waiting. The constable reappearing and requesting him with a quiet gravity which made the request an order not to leave the hall until further notice.

When they went along to the drawing room he was gone. Fenton brought in coffee, and in answer to Richard's question said he understood that a police car had arrived a few minutes ago, and that Mr Deane had left in it. He had, he added, sent a tray to Mr Deane in the hall.

'Then they must have arrested him,' said Lisa unhappily when Fenton had gone. 'If it were only interrogation, Mason could have questioned him here.'

'Not necessarily,' said Christopher. 'One must remember that he has probably given them a great deal of trouble by his outing, and they may want to impress their annoyance upon him.'

'There is a good deal of evidence against him. And he could, I suppose, have had a motive. We know that Uncle Mark left him five hundred pounds.' She didn't seem to notice Christopher's disapproving glance.

'We don't know that he knew that,' said Richard. 'I rather doubt if Mark would have told him. And it doesn't seem a hell of a lot to do murder for.'

Johnny gave Sally no warning glance, and she didn't need one. The Percival affair was not their secret.

The next hour and a quarter was wasted in an intermittent and uneasy discussion which got nowhere at all, and at three o'clock Fenton announced that Mason had arrived, and added, as a sort of aside, that Deane had come back with him. It seemed that Mason wanted to talk to Christopher, but Richard rose quickly and said: 'No. I'll see him first.' There was a brief argument, but Richard won, refusing even to let Christopher come with him.

When he had gone Christopher said: 'Well, since that's the way he wants it, there's something I'd like to say while he isn't here — I don't want to worry him about it. I realised from the first that we were going to have a bad time with the Press. Mercator's murder is news. Richard's return to life is also news. He by-passed the Press by coming home quietly before anyone expected him, and I gather he kept out of its clutches in town. He realised the danger, so he and Lisa kept pretty quiet.' Lisa nodded anxiously, and Christopher went on. 'Well, they know he's back now. I warned Fenton this morning and told him to see that both the gates were shut. But while we were upstairs he had to deal with two reporters who must have climbed the park wall. I gather he simply froze them off the doorstep. But we shall almost certainly have some more. Mason might be willing to help, but he obviously can't put a cordon round the grounds. So if you meet a reporter — any of you — please remember that the only safe answer is "No comment".'

Richard was with Mason for half an hour. Then the rest of them were called in, one by one, to confirm the fresh evidence and be taken through the statements they had made yesterday. Mason told them all that the inquest would be held at two o'clock tomorrow afternoon, and that, other things being equal, they would be free to leave Westwater when it was over.

It was after five when their interrogation ended. Deane hadn't come in for tea, and Lisa, with her Continental forthrightness, suggested that he should be summoned, told that everyone else had made a statement about his or her doings on the previous afternoon, and asked to do the same. But even Richard felt that this would be going a little too far, and finally, when Lisa pressed him, forbade her to do it. She obeyed reluctantly, and presently suggested a stroll in the garden. Christopher, probably in view of the Press, didn't seem very keen about it, but he came with the rest of them, and Sally noticed that he kept a fairly sharp look-out.

They moved together at first, but after a few minutes Lisa executed an unobtrusive and skilful manoeuvre which brought her to Sally's side, a little behind the others. She said quietly: 'There is something I want to ask you, Sally. After the inquest we shall be free to leave. I do not know what Richard will wish to do, but whatever he does I must be with him. But I cannot stay here with him unless there is a chaperone. Perhaps I, a German, attach more importance to this than you, an Englishwoman. But one must, at least, consider the possible feelings of Richard's neighbours, and I am asking you if you and Johnny, or at any rate you yourself, will stay with us for a little if Richard wishes to stay. It is not, of course, really for me to invite you. But I know that Richard would be very happy to have you. He likes you both very much.'

For a moment Sally didn't answer. The one thing she wanted was to go home with Johnny. But she knew she couldn't refuse.

'Yes, of course,' she said. 'I shall have to talk to Johnny — I don't quite know what his plans are — but I'm sure we can fix something.'

'Thank you,' said Lisa, and touched her hand.

The men were well ahead now. Lisa said miserably: 'I know that Richard did not do this thing. Not even in a moment of anger. He would never have struck an old man whom, in spite of everything, he loved. But I am so afraid the police will decide that he did it.'

'There's the Rover,' said Sally.

'That is true. And yet, Sally, I do not find it quite satisfactory to say that George did the murder. Richard has made it plain that he had no motive for a premeditated murder, and I do not think he has the temperament for an unpremeditated one. He is not an altogether admirable character — poor George — but he is not violent by nature.'

Sally thought privately that if George had been drinking heavily when he came down, he might quite easily have become violent. But she said: 'There isn't anyone else very likely, is there? We don't know about

Deane, of course. But Christopher had no possible motive, I imagine.'

'I wish I could be sure of that,' said Lisa very quietly.

Sally looked quickly at her. 'He only came down to talk business, surely.'

'Yes, I think so. He says Uncle Mark sent for him, just saying he wanted to talk business, and he presumes Uncle Mark wanted to give him his new will, to have it properly drawn up.'

'But they wouldn't have quarrelled about that. Surely not — even if Christopher had disapproved of the will.'

'I cannot be sure,' said Lisa. 'Sally, I must talk to someone of this. I could not speak of it this morning — I could not have spoken of it even if Christopher had not been there.' She clasped her hands tightly for a moment, and then let them fall to her sides.

'Richard said that Mark disliked me because he had a prejudice against Germans. That is true. But there was another reason. I think that because of his prejudice he was ready to think ill of me. When we were here on the day after Richard came home — just after you had left us, and before Richard and Mark went to the study — Richard went out of the room for a minute. As soon as he had gone, Mark told me a horrible thing. He told me he had discovered that I was Christopher's mistress.'

Sally found herself quite unable to comment.

'It was not true,' said Lisa simply. 'Christopher was in love with me and had asked me to marry him. I had seen a good deal of him — he was very kind to me after Richard was shot down. That was all. But it was no use arguing — Mark had decided. He told me I must give up Richard, or he would tell Richard what he knew. I said I couldn't do that because it was not true. But this was why I tried to break off our engagement. Richard

was already angry with Christopher, because he had
seen that Christopher was in love with me — we were
at his office last week — and I was afraid he would believe Mark.'

'I see,' said Sally inadequately. 'Do you mean you
think Mark might have accused Christopher of this?'

'I think he might have told Christopher that it was
his reason for making the new will. And since the
murder may have been unpremeditated…'

She went on after a moment. 'And, Sally, have you
thought that it would have been easier for Christopher
than for anyone else to hide the will in the Telephone
Directory? Johnny said this morning that it was
Christopher who telephoned for the police and the
doctor. Johnny said it — Christopher himself did not
remind us of it.'

'But why should he have hidden it at all?' asked
Sally.

'I could see no reason at first. But this morning,
after the will had been discovered, he said to Richard
and me that he thought the clause about me could almost certainly be set aside. It seems that the tendency
in the English courts of law is to set aside clauses which
are what he calls "in restraint of marriage". Now, he
would probably not have been able to form this
opinion in a moment, and so — not knowing that
Richard had seen the will — he might have argued in
this way. If, after studying it carefully, he decided that
there was little or no hope of setting aside the restraining clause, it would be better to destroy the will.
Richard would not in any case give me up, and by de-
stroying it Christopher would spare us some distress,
and himself, perhaps, the embarrassment of explaining
why Mark had made such a will. It might even be more
than an embarrassment, for if I told the truth it might
suggest that he had had a motive for…violence. If, on

the other hand, he saw a fair chance of setting the clause aside, he must in justice to us allow the will to be found — in a place where anyone might have put it. He could not, of course, run the risk of remaining in the study to read it. But he could have read it in the drawing room — and then, what more easy for Mark's solicitor than to take it upon himself to ring up the police?'

Sally suppressed the reply that all this would be highly unprofessional conduct. Possibly a lawyer who had already committed murder wouldn't worry about being professional. But she was rescued at this point by the Colonel, who came back to take his leave.

They saw him to his car and watched him drive off down the west avenue. He had gone a couple of hundred yards when a young man emerged from the shrubbery on the far side from the garden and made hopeful signs to him.

'Damn!' said Christopher with a surprisingly human fervour. 'That's a reporter. Go back to the house. I'll try to prevent Danby from talking to him.'

The reporter had now started talking to Danby. The Colonel's face was thrust out of the window, and it seemed even redder than usual. As Christopher moved towards him, he gave a bellow and opened his door.

Richard said sharply: 'Lisa and Sally, go back,' and broke into a run. Johnny followed him. Sally saw Christopher quicken his pace, and then saw that Danby's fist was raised.

It was difficult to tell exactly what happened. She thought the reporter dodged, and Danby's blow went wide. But the other men confused her view. Then they were on either side of the Colonel, and everyone was talking at once. Sally looked at Lisa and saw that she was rather shaken. 'We'd better go back, Lisa,' she said.

Johnny and Richard and Christopher re-joined

them ten minutes later. Lisa said quickly: 'He didn't hurt him, Richard?'

'No,' said Richard briefly. 'It's all right, darling.'

Johnny changed the subject by telling Sally that Richard wanted them to finish sorting out the libraries, a job which would have to be finished in any case. They were to let the valuation go for the moment. Johnny thought they had better get on with the sorting now.

As soon as they were in the library Sally asked: 'What happened?'

'The reporter evidently introduced himself as representing the *Sunday Echo* — which, of course, was enough to annoy a staunch and conventional Conservative. Then, when Danby refused to talk, he was unwise enough to mention a sum of money. I don't think he can be very experienced.'

'Probably not,' said Sally. 'But you might come clean. Richard was afraid Danby might get violent. Why? How did he know? Danby's got a temper, but you wouldn't expect him to hit complete strangers, however annoying. And Lisa knew something too.'

'Yes,' said Johnny. 'Richard wouldn't have reacted so sharply if his nerves hadn't been on edge, but he had some reason for being worried. Christopher prised it out of him after Danby and the reporter had gone. Danby was wounded in the head about twenty-five years ago, somewhere in India, and ever since then he's been given to occasional violence. When Richard was a schoolboy, he saw him knock out a poacher who was operating on his land. So he's rather naturally been worrying ever since he heard that Danby was found standing over the body. He dreamt about the poacher incident last night. He confided in Lisa this morning, but he wasn't going to confide in anyone else, and he refuses to let anyone tell the police. He says it's very likely they know already — and looking back to some of Mason's questions I'm inclined to agree with him — and even if they don't it isn't evidence.'

'I can't believe Mark knew it,' said Sally after a moment.

'No. I'm quite sure he'd never have baited Danby if he had. After all, he'd only been living here a very short time.' Johnny frowned. 'But this rather invalidates my theory about the underlying discipline of Army men.'

Sally agreed. Then she remembered her conversation with Lisa. Johnny wasn't very pleased by the prospect of staying on at Westwater but said it would have to be arranged. On their original estimate they wouldn't have finished their job before the end of this week, so he wasn't expected back before next Monday. He refused in any case to consider letting Sally stay on without him.

He listened to Lisa's suggestions about Christopher and said he didn't take much stock in them. 'Even if he were accused of being Lisa's lover, I doubt very much if he'd offer violence, especially to a much older man. And I find her will theory very hard to take seriously. But of course she's a foreigner, and she probably doesn't know much about English lawyers. What does interest me is the production of a much more likely motive for Mercator's attitude to her. I wasn't really satisfied by the Germanophobe theory. Mercator might have tried to break up the engagement because he disliked Germans, but I couldn't quite see him going as far as to cut Richard out of his will. But Jews can be exceptionally rigid on the question of chastity. If he believed Lisa had been another man's mistress, he would probably go all lengths to prevent the marriage.' He stopped. 'But we're being paid to sort out libraries, not to investigate murders.'

* * *

IN SPITE OF EVERYTHING, the spell of their work took hold of them again. Sally couldn't forget the tragedy which was being played out beyond the library, but they helped each other to concentrate, and gradually the work filled more and more of her mind. She almost jumped when the door opened and someone stumbled on the threshold.

'Hullo, Deane,' said Johnny, coming to the surface.

Deane stammered for a moment, and then said with a slight gasp: 'Would you mind if I talked to you?'

'Not at all,' said Johnny. 'Come along.'

'Would you rather talk to Johnny in private?' asked Sally, coming down from the library ladder.

'Oh, no, please, Mrs Heldar. I'd like you — that is, I think you know something about it as well as Mr Heldar.' He looked at her like an eager, anxious dog, and she understood that he really wanted her to stay.

They sat down, and Johnny passed round cigarettes. When everyone had a light he looked at Deane and said: 'Well?'

Deane said jerkily: 'I've been very upset. I'm in serious trouble with the police, and I don't know what to do. Miss Harz wanted me to tell her what I was doing yesterday afternoon, but I couldn't talk to her. But I thought it over for a bit and I thought perhaps I could tell you. It — it was you who found out about the Percival, wasn't it?' He stuck for a moment, and then said desperately: 'Well, it was I who took it.'

He launched out into a long and muddled explanation of his financial difficulties. It appeared that as Mercator's secretary he had acquired a certain amount of information about the Stock Exchange and had been tempted to indulge in what he called 'a little flutter'. He hadn't liked to ask Mercator's advice, knowing that Mercator strongly disapproved of little flutters by people who had nothing but their salaries, but four months ago he had run into an old acquaintance of his called Landon, who was now an outside broker, and with Landon's assistance had fluttered a little with moderate success. But he had been buying on a margin — a system which Sally had to have explained by Johnny afterwards — and after his third flutter had found himself obliged to raise something like a hundred pounds before the next settling day. He hadn't dared to ask Mercator for help, and he had nothing of sufficient value to sell or pawn. It was at this point that he had thought of selling one of Mercator's more valuable books.

The degrees of casuistry with which he had soothed his conscience were tiresome and rather pitiful. He might someday be able to buy the book back and restore it to the library, and anyway books weren't much use to a man who was half blind. If suspicion fell on Richard Thaxton, Thaxton was dead and it couldn't hurt him. The whole thing had happened very much as Johnny had worked it out. He had found the reprint after some difficulty, and then sold the First Edition to Mumford. He had had the sense to see that it would be dangerous to ask for a cash payment but had felt that it would be equally dangerous to give his own name, so, a little coolly, he had given Landon's. Landon, confronted half an hour later with a cheque for ninety-five pounds, made out to himself by a man he had never heard of, had at first been inclined to ask questions, but had subsequently accepted a vague and unconvincing explanation, possibly on the ground that it would be safer for him not to know the truth.

But Deane had obviously not been intended for a criminal. The news of Richard's return to life had shaken him badly. He had been prepared for an ultimate discovery of the forgery, but the information that the Heldars were coming down in two days' time had been another serious shock. He had become more and more nervous and unhappy until, when Mercator had summoned him on the morning after their arrival and charged him directly with the substitution, he had been almost relieved.

'He said I'd been a damned fool, but he was very generous about it. He said he'd known at once that I'd done it, because I'd been so jumpy lately, and because Squadron Leader Thaxton was about the only other possible person, and he knew he wouldn't have done it. He said he'd work out some way of getting the Percival back, and then he would stop four pounds a month from my salary until I'd repaid him. I expect he'd have worked out his plan by the next day if it hadn't been for his accident. But he didn't have it ready until yesterday. Yesterday morning he dictated a letter to me.' Deane repeated the substance of the letter which Mason had shown to the Heldars.

'I was to have taken it to Mr Mumford today. I typed it after lunch, and just after three I took it along to the study to get it signed. The police have been asking me about that today, and I told them the truth. I hadn't mentioned it before because I was afraid they'd pick on me. But now they say someone saw me. Someone seems to have said I went into the study. But I didn't. Just as I got to the door I remembered that Squadron Leader Thaxton or Mr Sheringham might be with Sir Mark, and I listened to hear if he was talking to anyone. I heard him say: 'Nothing you can say will alter my decision.' He said it quite quietly, but there was something — well, sort of final about it. I don't know who he was talking to; I didn't hear any answer. I went back to my room and decided to leave the letter till after tea. And then the police found it on my desk, and I think they suspected that I'd written it and left it about to show that I had no motive for murdering Sir Mark.'

'Did you admit the substitution?' asked Johnny.

'No. I — I said that what Sir Mark had said in the letter was true — that I sold the Percival on his instructions.'

'That was damned silly,' said Johnny succinctly. 'And how did you explain the cheque to Landon?'

'Well, I said it was late in the afternoon when I went to Mumford's — about half-past five — which was quite true. I needed some ready cash, and the banks were shut. So I gave Landon's name, knowing that he would advance me some money on the cheque that afternoon. I thought it wiser to give a false name, anyway.'

'And then you had to get in touch with Landon before the police did and ask him to tell the same story.'

Deane had given the police Landon's office address, saying he had no idea where Landon lived, and Mason had evidently not thought it worthwhile to go further into the matter that evening. But it had been impossible to ring up from Westwater; a constable had remained in the hall all night, with the door of the telephone room in full view, and in any case, Deane mistrusted the Danesfield exchange. So he had caught the seven-forty-five bus and rung up Landon's house from a call box in Fanchester, and Landon had agreed, reluctantly, to support his story. He had then waited till the banks opened, and cashed a cheque, so that he could, if necessary, give an account of his outing which would bear investigation. He had had to wait for the eleven-thirty bus to Danesfield but had got into the house without being seen. Questioned by Mason in the afternoon, he had stuck obstinately to the bank story. Mason had been obstinately sceptical.

'So what am I to do?' asked Deane, with an unhappy, childlike simplicity.

'Well, you've asked for my advice,' said Johnny. 'Go

and tell the constable in the hall that you want to tell Mason the truth. And then do it.'

'But if admit I took the Percival—'

'My good fool,' began Johnny, and then collected himself. 'Now listen. Mason knows perfectly well that you took the Percival. He asked us about the substitution, and it was perfectly obvious that he had no doubt you were responsible. So he knows you're lying about that. He obviously knows you're lying when you say you went into Fanchester merely to visit your bank; it's about the least convincing story I've ever heard. Why would you want cash when you can't even go to the village shop? Very well. If he knows you're lying about all that, how the hell do you expect him to believe you when you say that you didn't make up the letter yourself, and that you didn't go into the study yesterday afternoon?'

Deane saw the force of that. Johnny elicited the final fact that the Percival had been collected by the police from Jimmy Mumford, who hadn't got round to selling it, and then pointed out that Richard as well as Mason would have to know the truth. But Deane seemed quite incapable of telling Richard, and at last Johnny agreed to do it for him before the police did. Then, unhappy but reasonably determined, he went to find the constable.

Johnny sighed, and lit another cigarette. 'He hasn't got the guts of a sparrow,' he said, 'but I hope and believe he's telling the truth now.'

'Gloria did say he went into the study.'

'Not quite. She said she saw him "just going in". If you see a man standing outside a door — perhaps even with his hand on the handle — you naturally assume that he's going in. You may be wrong. I'd like to question Gloria further about that, but it's not really my business. Mason will do it.'

* * *

DEANE'S second departure in a police car worried Richard so much that after dinner Johnny took him and Sally into the library and told him the story there and then. He was on the whole relieved.

'If this is true,' he said, 'then it was Mark's wish that no action should be taken against him, and so, of course, it's mine too. After all, he was Mark's man. I'll see him when he gets back, and I'll talk to Mason about it. Thank you very much, Johnny; I'm most grateful.'

'We only listened to him,' said Johnny. 'Now, I think perhaps, if you'll forgive us, we'll stay and do a little more work.'

They worked for three-quarters of an hour or so, but Johnny was slightly *distrait*. Finally he said: 'You get on with the job for a little while, if you don't mind, darling. I've got something I want to work out.'

He sat down at the table and took a sheet of the foolscap they were using. Sally, looking over his shoulder, saw him head it: 'DEANE'S EVIDENCE'.

'We're being paid to sort out libraries,' she said, 'not to investigate murders.'

'That,' said Johnny, 'will be quite enough from you.'

Sally kissed the top of his head, and he pulled her down to him. After a moment he said: 'We're not being paid for that either. Go to it, darling.'

He didn't speak again for nearly an hour. Then he asked her to come and look, and she read what he had written.

DEANE'S EVIDENCE

Deane states that he was outside the door of the study at approximately 3.5 pm on the day of the murder, and that he heard Mercator say: 'Nothing you can say will alter my decision.'

These words could have been applied to any of the known suspects: to Richard, with regard to the will; to Christopher, with regard to the will, which he might have been opposing; to George, with regard to the line Mercator was taking with Richard about the land-agency; a little less plausibly to Danby, with regard to the line Mercator had said he would take with Richard about the farm — it seems rather unlikely that Mercator would have been 'quieter' and 'final' about a matter which he looked on more or less as a joke. Or to Deane himself, with regard to a decision to dismiss or even to prosecute him for the theft of the Percival. We have still no proof that Mercator hadn't come to such a decision, and Deane could have reported words which were actually spoken to him, while inventing the context. In the case of any other murderer, his statement can reasonably be accepted.

* * *

Richard. If Richard is the murderer, it was presumably he to whom Mercator was speaking at 3.5. He could have murdered Mercator at any time between 3.5 and, possibly, 3.40, when he might still have left the house without being seen or heard, and which would still have given him time to reach Lisa's flat by 5.45. *But* what about the Rover? It seems unlikely that Danby is mistaken in stating that he saw it.

It might, I think, be possible to make out a case for premeditated murder against Richard on the assumption that, in order to confuse the issue, and perhaps to incriminate George, he used both the Armstrong and the Rover, driving away in the Armstrong at 2.45, returning on foot or in the Rover to commit the murder, and subsequently driving away in the Rover. But this would almost certainly involve an accomplice (? Lisa) to drive one of the cars back to town, if not also to bring the Rover down, and any such case would seem to break down on the fact that Richard would certainly expect Christopher to be with Mercator when he returned. Since he didn't know that Christopher would be at Westwater until he arrived there himself, he might have planned such a murder, but it is difficult to see how he could have carried it out.

Christopher. If Christopher is the murderer, it was presumably he to whom Mercator was speaking at 3.5. He could have murdered Mercator at any time between 3.5 and, say, 3.40, and would then have had only to slip back to the drawing room — probably by way of the garden, as he wouldn't want to risk being seen in the house or passing the library windows — and await developments. *But* what about the Rover?

George. If George is the murderer, it was presumably he to whom Mercator was speaking at 3.5. He could have committed the murder at any time between 3.5 and, say, 3.20, the time depending upon whether he had brought the Rover up to the house or left it at some little distance, since it was seen at the west gate at 3.25. There is no evidence to indicate which of these courses he may have taken; no one appears to have heard the Rover in the neighbourhood of the house, but then no one appears to have heard Danby's car, which we know was within earshot at one point. If the murder was premeditated — which in George's case seems unlikely — he would almost certainly have concealed the Rover at some little distance. Danby's statement makes it clear that he did not see it turn out of the west gate; it could, therefore, have been ahead of him on the road for some little way. It may be worth noting that George, as ex-land-agent, must be familiar with the neighbourhood, and would therefore know of a suitable place to leave the Rover, concealed or not.

Danby. If Danby is the murderer, we cannot assume that it was he to whom Mercator was speaking at 3.5. In this case he may well have invented the Rover in order to incriminate Richard and may therefore have reached the west gate before 3.25, and there is, apparently, no evidence apart from his own that he visited the farm before coming up to the house. But it seems a little unlikely that he would quarrel with Mercator for half an hour or so before murdering him, and even more unlikely that he would remain in the study for more than a few minutes after murdering him. Therefore, if he had been there at 3.5, we should probably not have found him there at approximately 3.46. It is conceivable that *(a)* Deane in fact entered the study at 3.5, *(b)* Christopher was with Mercator, *(c)* Richard was still there; any one of them, although innocent of murder, might be lying to avoid incrimination. Or, if Danby's statement about the Rover is true, it is conceivable that *(d)* George was there.

In view of the time factor, however, it is a little difficult to suppose that Danby arrived before, say, 3.15 at the earliest. If we are to believe Richard when he says he left at 2.45, Mercator would almost certainly have fetched Christopher by 3.15, if he had been alive to do so. It is therefore a little unlikely that Danby committed the murder at all.

Deane. If Deane is the murderer, his statement is presumably false. He presumably entered the study at

3.5 and could have committed the murder at any time between 3.5 and, say, 3.40. It is more likely, however, that he committed it within a few minutes of 3.5, since Mercator would almost certainly be reluctant to keep Christopher waiting in order to talk to his own secretary. It is, indeed, a little unlikely that he committed it at all, since — again if Richard's statement is to be accepted — Mercator would probably have fetched Christopher by 3.5 if he had been alive to do so. It might, however, be as well to consider in this case the possibility that Mercator had been so shaken by his interview with Richard that he wanted a little time alone to recover from it. *But* what about the Rover?

* * *

NB. This scheme is submitted in total ignorance of the medical evidence, but it seems unlikely that the medical evidence will substantially alter the picture as we see it here. Whether Deane's evidence is true or false, we can be fairly certain that Mercator did not die before 3.5. A *terminus ad quern* before 3.30 would tend to establish the innocence of Danby.

'I don't know that it gets us much further,' said Johnny, 'but it makes one thing fairly clear. Unless the Rover is a pure coincidence — unless George just happened to come down here yesterday without murdering Mercator — we have got to take it into consideration. And there are only two likely theories which explain the Rover: (*a*) that George is the murderer, and (*b*) that Danby is the murderer, in which case he would have a motive for inventing the Rover.'

'I think George is the more likely.'

Johnny nodded. 'Danby may be given to violence,

but I think he's an entirely honest man. If he had killed Mercator, I doubt very much if he'd try to throw suspicion on anyone else — and particularly on Richard, whom he seems to be fond of. And I don't want to give a dog a bad name and hang him, but we have to remember that of all these people George is the only one who is a really unsatisfactory character.'

CHAPTER SIX

George Willesdon arrived just before lunch the next day. Everyone was a little shaken by his appearance, the more so since he walked into the drawing room unannounced, giving no chance to Fenton, who hovered behind him, obviously unhappy and outraged.

'Well, Dick!' he said cheerfully. 'It's good to see you again, old boy. You didn't seem so keen to meet your old friends in town, but when a man comes back to a girl like Lisa, one must make allowances, mustn't one?' He slapped Richard heartily on the back, and kissed Lisa on both cheeks.

They bore it extremely well. Richard greeted him with some appearance of warmth and made introductions. For a moment George seemed slightly embarrassed by the presence of the Heldars, but he made a quick recovery.

'Delighted to see you again, Mrs Heldar. I put up a bit of a black last time we met, didn't I? Sorry about that. But now we can make a fresh start, can't we?' His eyes, taking her in, were openly appreciative; there was no subtlety about George. Or was there? thought Sally uncomfortably. Then he shook hands with Johnny. 'Well, Heldar, old boy. No ill-feeling, I hope?'

Sally decided that George had been too tight on his last visit to remember much about it. He was also very slightly tight now. Otherwise, surely, he couldn't be so entirely brazen. She found it increasingly difficult to believe that this was really the same young man.

He greeted Christopher with the same heartiness and met with a definitely cold reception. Then he looked hopefully at the tray of drinks. But Richard handled him with considerable skill, giving him a glass of sherry, and as soon as lunch was announced, asking him to bring it with him. They were lunching early, Richard explained, because of the inquest.

It was Christopher who asked him if he was a witness. He raised his eyebrows very high, and said: 'Oh, no. I couldn't tell them anything about the murder. I just came to stand by old Dick. Thought he might like an old friend about, you know. As a matter of fact, I was in Fanchester anyway, so I came out by the eleven-thirty bus. This police chap — Mason, isn't he? — wanted to ask me about one or two things. The little affair the other evening, and so on. But I couldn't help him much.'

Richard's behaviour was quite admirable. It would have been impossible not to support him, and lunch went a great deal better than might have been expected. George himself seemed sublimely unconscious of any lack of warmth in his welcome.

They started for the village just after ten to two; Christopher had insisted that they shouldn't be early, because the Press would certainly be there in force. Richard was driving Lisa and Fenton in the Armstrong, and Johnny put Sally into it too, and firmly manoeuvred George into his own car, with Christopher and Deane. Richard, who knew the way, led them.

Danesfield was a tiny place, and the inquest was to be held in the public bar of the Thaxton Arms. There was a little crowd round the doorway. Some of the people were local, but some were obviously reporters. Sally recognised the young man from the *Sunday Echo*. Then Richard turned into the inn yard. He drew up and said: 'Quick, everybody. Back door.'

They almost did it. But as they approached the door they seemed to be suddenly surrounded by a press of reporters.

'Good afternoon, Mr Thaxton. If we might just have a statement—'

'How did they treat you in China, Squadron Leader?'

'Just a minute, Mr Thaxton.'

There was a sudden flash of light. Then the door opened, a friendly red face appeared, and a deep voice said: 'Come on, Mr Richard.'

Richard swept Lisa in, and the others followed. Sally felt Johnny's hand on her arm.

The proceedings might have been more trying than they were. The police had evidently decided that as little evidence as possible should be brought, and the Coroner, a lawyer from Fanchester, had evidently agreed with them. Apart from police and medical witnesses, only a few people were called. There was Danby, self-important and inclined to be garrulous. There was Fenton, low-voiced and respectful. There was Johnny, very quiet and convincing. And there was Richard, who identified the body, looking thinner than ever in a suit which must date from before his imprisonment, white-faced and painfully haggard, giving his evidence in a steady, expressionless voice.

Richard had insisted on giving evidence. He might have been spared the ordeal — as it had turned out, the police surgeon had pronounced him unfit for interrogation — and Christopher as well as Lisa had been disapproving and apprehensive. Christopher had pointed out that if, as was perfectly possible, the appearance of the Rover was not brought in evidence, and if, as was very likely, Richard's quarrel with Mark was, an igno-rant country jury might receive the impression that there was a case against Richard. Richard had laughed heartily for the first time in Sally's experience and told Christopher gently that there was a case against him.

The Rover was not mentioned, and the quarrel was elicited from Richard, who admitted it frankly. But no one need have worried. The jury listened solemnly to the evidence, withdrew, returned after a few minutes, and delivered itself of a verdict of murder against a person or persons unknown. The elderly foreman added gravely: 'An' we would like to say, sir, that Mr Richard Thaxton 'as all our sympathy in the tragic death of 'is uncle, 'oo we all looked up to an' respected.'

They were mobbed again by the reporters on the way out, and the situation was made the more painful by the behaviour of George. He had followed them through the crowd to the cars, and Christopher, per-haps unwisely, laid a hand on his arm and said in a low voice: 'Look here, Willesdon; Richard's had about enough. I'm going to try to make him rest. So if you don't mind, perhaps it would be better if you didn't come back.'

'Okay, old boy,' said George, resignedly but clearly. 'I know when I'm not wanted. I'll stick around here and have a drink with the Press boys.'

The Westwater party was silent for a moment. Then Richard said quietly: 'Come back and have some tea, George.'

George had some tea, and discussed the inquest cheerfully and at length, and with a fine disregard for everyone's feelings, until nearly half-past five. Then he glanced at the clock and said: 'Look, Dick, old boy, I've missed the five-ten bus. Could you be a good chap and let me have the Rover to get me back to town?'

This time the silence seemed frozen. Richard broke it, saying with admirable calm: 'I'm sorry, George, but the Rover isn't here.'

George's eyebrows went up again. 'Not here?' he said. 'I thought you brought her down on Monday.'

'No. I came down in Lisa's Armstrong.'

'Why did you think Richard came down in the Rover?' asked Christopher incisively.

'Well, she was gone when I went to take her out,' said George. His tone was a shade too innocent to be true. 'I rang up Lisa's flat a little before twelve, and she said Dick had just started for Westwater. I wanted to see him — you'll admit you weren't very easy to come at in town, Dick — and it was damned hot, and I thought it would be nice to get out into the country for a bit. I imagined you'd taken Lisa's car — after all, it would be on the spot — so I went along to the mews. That was about a quarter past twelve. But the lock-up was empty. So naturally I thought you'd got the old lady. The police asked me about that too. Someone saw me go into the lock-up and told them — it must have been young Fenwick; you remember, Lisa; the pub-lisher type who has the flat opposite your old one. He passed me just as I was going in. So I told them the cup-board was bare. Couldn't do anything else. I left it at that — the resources didn't run to a railway fare and anyway it wasn't worth it — and I went and lunched at a Lyons' and on to the pictures for a bit and had tea at another Lyons'. That's about all I can rise to nowadays.'

'I see,' said Richard. There was a long pause, and Sally saw the increasing strain in his face. Then he said: 'Look, George — I'll send you into Fanchester. Morley will take you. Do you mind if he takes the Armstrong, Lisa? Mark always said he was a first-class chauffeur.'

'Of course not, darling.'

'Fine,' said George. 'Fine. Thanks, Dick.'

Richard rang the bell and made his request to Fenton. It was noticeable that he never gave orders to the servants, though whether this was because they were not his servants, or simply a part of his natural courtesy, Sally wasn't quite sure.

'I am sorry, Mr Richard,' said Fenton. 'It is Morley's afternoon off. He went into Fanchester by the five-ten bus, to visit his mother.'

'I see, Fenton. Thank you.'

Sally saw that Johnny was about to offer to drive George. But Christopher got in first.

'I'll take you, Willesdon,' he said. 'Come along, and I'll get my car out.'

The offer was evidently prompted by sympathy for Richard. But Christopher spoke a little too shortly.

'That's very good of you, Christopher,' said Richard.

George smiled, not very pleasantly. 'No real hurry, is there, Sheringham?' he asked. 'I don't think there's a train till about ten to seven.'

'I want to get back as soon as possible, if you don't mind.'

Lisa looked at Richard's chalk-white face, and said almost sharply: 'Please, George. Richard and Christopher have things to discuss.'

'I'm sure they have,' said George. 'Poor old Dick's not in a very nice position, is he?'

Lisa rose up and faced him. 'You are not perhaps in a very nice position yourself, George,' she said gently. 'Now please go.'

George gave an exaggerated shrug. 'Okay, okay, I'll go. I told you before: I know when I'm not wanted.

People who come out of concentration camps are apt to be a bit touchy. *I* know.'

Christopher moved over to the door, opened it, and waited.

'I'm coming,' said George. 'Goodbye, Dick, old boy. Goodbye, Lisa; see you some more. Let's dine at Emil's again one night; I'm sure Dick would enjoy it. Even Sheringham approves of it, doesn't he? The food's good, and old Emil's always full of reminiscences. And I've got a new after-dinner story.'

As the door closed behind him, Lisa went quickly over to Richard and took his hands. She was as white as he was, and there were tears in her eyes. Sally didn't blame her. She was almost crying with rage herself.

* * *

THE HELDARS WERE thankful to retire to the library. They didn't hold an indignation meeting; it was rather too bad for that. Only, when Sally asked Johnny a little later what he thought of George as a suspect now that he had met him, Johnny replied that he almost hoped George would be arrested whether he was guilty or not. Then he became a little more reasonable.

'I don't honestly know what I think,' he said. 'I have the impression that George is a pretty simple type — not quite as simple as he chooses to appear, but definitely not subtle. Well, that's all right. The murder needn't have been subtle, even if it was premeditated. And George's defence, if he did it, is not subtle. He's told his story and he's sticking to it. It has the advantage of being perfectly straightforward, reasonably plausible, and probably quite impossible to disprove, unless someone actually saw him in the Westwater neighbourhood. The only thing that makes it a little suspicious — apart from the fact that Richard was driving the Armstrong that day — is all these Lyonses and pictures. If you can't prove an alibi, the next best thing is to swear you were somewhere where no one is at all likely to be able to say you weren't.' He paused and began to light a pipe. 'George's essential quality is brazenness. He probably lives by it. He's trying to carry off this situation by it, whether he did the murder or not.'

'Could anyone be so brazen if he had done the murder?'

'I ask myself that too. I just don't know.'

Three-quarters of an hour later Christopher put his head round the door. His face was a little red, and his forehead damp.

'Shall I disturb you if I come in for a little while?' he asked. 'I don't want to bother Lisa and Richard if they're in the drawing room.'

'Come along,' said Johnny. 'You look as if you needed to cool off.'

'Thank you.' Christopher collapsed into a chair and mopped at his brow. 'As a matter of fact, Fenton saw me come in and suggested beer, and I asked him to bring it in here. I believe the man's human after all.'

Sally smiled. She had been thinking precisely the same thing about Christopher himself.

'You've earned it,' she said.

'I believe I have. I have never in my life passed a more unpleasant half-hour. Willesdon was offensive, boastful, and sorry for himself, sometimes by turns and sometimes all at once. He told me all about his life and hard times. He told me all about the wonderful job he's going to get. He told me all about how he escaped from his Oflag-Luft in 'forty-four. It was a long story, but I suspect that it boiled down to a bit of luck and the fact that he was so appallingly brazen about it that the Germans didn't notice when he left. Possibly that's why he labours under the delusion that being brazen will get him anywhere he wants to go.'

'Possibly it is,' said Johnny thoughtfully.

The door opened, and Fenton appeared with a heavily loaded tray. Sally saw her husband observe with satisfaction that it held several bottles and several tumblers. At the same moment Richard's voice said from the terrace: 'Do I see beer? May I join the party?' He walked in. 'Lisa's lying down — she's got a headache.'

'No wonder,' said Christopher under his breath.

A discreet cough sounded, and Richard turned. 'Yes, Fenton?'

Fenton was looking a little anxious. 'Excuse me, Mr Richard,' he said. 'There is a person on the telephone asking for you — from Fanchester. I understood him to say that he was a member of your old squadron, but I could not catch his name, and I am not satisfied that he was trying to pronounce it intelligibly. It is possible that he is genuine, but I suspect that he may be a representative of the Press.'

'I'll go,' said Christopher quickly, and got up.

'No, you won't, Christopher,' said Richard. 'I'll take it myself.' He went out before Christopher had time to argue.

When he came back his face was hard and angry. 'It was the Press,' he said shortly, and Sally was glad that Christopher refrained from saying: 'I told you so.'

* * *

RICHARD HAD EVIDENTLY DECIDED to stay on at Westwater at any rate until after his uncle's funeral, for which the authorities had now given permission. It was to take place on Friday, and the arrangements were being made by Mercator's partner and Jewish executor. Christopher, who also had responsibilities as an executor, and was in any case needed at his office, left for London early on the morning after the inquest. The others were to go up on Friday, although in accordance with Jewish practice only the men would attend the funeral.

Sally hoped for everyone's sake that Thursday would be a quiet day. The Heldars went downstairs a little after half-past nine and had settled down to work when Lisa came in to say good morning. She looked as if she hadn't slept much. She said she thought Richard would be down in a few minutes and was on the point of going out again when hurried footsteps sounded on the terrace.

They seemed to pause briefly at one of the drawing room windows, and then came quickly on. Sally heard harsh, laboured breathing. Then the Colonel appeared at the window, with the sweat running down his scarlet face.

'Thank Heaven,' he said, gasping. 'Thought no one was about. Heldar — there's a man in Mercator's dam. Think it's Willesdon — can't be sure. He's almost certainly dead — probably been in the water for hours — but we must get him out. Probably the best way for him, but one must try. Come on. Get a couple of gardeners and — some rope.'

'Sally or Lisa,' said Johnny, 'ring up Hill's house and see if you can get a message to him. He must come straight to the dam. Then ring up Mason and tell him. The bobby's not here this morning.'

'Johnny!' said Lisa quickly, and put a hand on his arm. 'Richard must not know, or he will want to go with you — and he must not go. It would be so bad for him. Could you not stay and talk to him — talk business or something — so that he shall not guess anything

is wrong? Send the head gardener — he is a countryman — he will know what to do. I am so tired this
morning, and Richard knows me so well — I could not
conceal it from him.'

'I'm sorry,' said Johnny quietly. 'I must go. If Sally
can help you, she will. Please do that telephoning at
once.'

Then he and Danby went out by the window, and
Sally and Lisa were left looking at each other. Sally
thought that Lisa really didn't look capable of tackling
Richard. But after a minute her head went up.

'I must wait for Richard,' she said. 'Will you telephone, Sally?'

Hill was out, but his wife said she would do her best
to get hold of him. Mason was immediately available.
He received the news quietly and said he would send an
ambulance and come out himself. He added gravely:
'I'm sorry, Mrs Heldar. Another nasty shock for you.
Don't worry too much.'

She didn't know if Richard had come down or not.
She went out by the front door and wandered about the
lawn. Ten minutes later Lisa came slowly round the end
of the west wing and joined her.

'He has gone,' she said.

It was after half-past eleven when the men came
back. Their faces made it perfectly clear that the man in
the dam had been George, and that George was dead.

'But,' said Lisa presently, 'why should he have come
back here? He was going to London.' It was a question
which she and Sally had already discussed without ar-
riving at any reasonable answer.

'We don't know,' said Richard. 'We may never know.
But he probably came back on the seven-five bus.
Christopher must have left him at the station — or put
him down somewhere in Fanchester — a little after six,
and he must have changed his mind in the interval. He

was in the Arms between half-past eight and nine — the Colonel saw him. I think Mason's making enquiries there now. I'm afraid he'll be up here soon — he says he's got to get statements from everybody who saw George yesterday.'

Mason arrived about half-past twelve and interviewed first Lisa and then Sally. He seemed to be principally concerned with getting a picture of George's state of mind on the previous day. Then he saw Deane, and then — a little surprisingly, for he had taken the other men's statements at the dam — Danby, who had to be summoned from the dining room, where they were pretending to have lunch. The Colonel, when he returned, seemed slightly ill at ease, but said nothing about his interview. Richard went out for a moment to see Mason and came back with a little more news.

'Mason's seen Wainwright — that's the landlord of the Arms, who let us in at the back door yesterday. Wainwright says George did come back on the seven-five. He had some supper and booked a room for the night. He went up to bed soon after closing time but in the morning he was gone.'

'Poor old Wainwright must have thought he'd been bilked,' said Danby. 'I daresay he only took Willesdon in because he was a friend of yours; he knew him only too well. I suppose the feller was tight by closing time?'

'Mason didn't say. But I think you said he wasn't tight when you saw him?'

'He wasn't stone-cold sober. He'd had one or two. But he wasn't really tight — strange to say,' said the Colonel irritably. Then he broke off. 'Ah, well. I suppose we shouldn't speak ill of the dead — even under these circumstances. But I fancy the case is closed.'

Christopher, who arrived about five o'clock, after visiting Fanchester to make his contribution to the evidence, seemed to be of the same opinion.

* * *

THE DAY of the funeral was rather tiring and, even for Sally, rather painful. She spent most of the afternoon in Lisa's very comfortable and attractive flat in Chelsea. Lisa was unhappy, but she couldn't altogether conceal her profound relief. Richard seemed to be safe, and that was all that really mattered to her. Sally could understand that, but for some obscure reason she couldn't quite share Lisa's impression — which seemed to be a general one — that everything was over bar the shouting. There would be the inquest on George, probably on Monday, and then the case would be closed. Everything pointed to George as the murderer, George as the suicide because he was the murderer. It was unreasonable to keep on wondering if anyone could have been so brazen if he had done the murder, if George's behaviour on Wednesday had really been the behaviour of a man who might break suddenly and decide to give up a hopeless struggle.

After dinner the Heldars took refuge in the library again. There was no real need to work, for the weekend would give them plenty of time to finish the job, but it seemed better to leave Richard and Lisa alone. They were a little surprised when, just before ten o'clock, Richard joined them.

'I hope you don't mind,' he said. 'I've sent Lisa to bed — she's very tired — and I'd rather like a talk with you both.'

He sat down in one of the big chairs, obviously quite unconscious of the startling effect of his white, fine-boned face against the dark leather. A Thaxton painted by Sargent, thought Sally. He passed round cigarettes, and then seemed to have some difficulty in opening the conversation. But he didn't make small talk. He looked out of the open window for a few moments, and then turned directly to Johnny and Sally and began.

'This is an awkward question,' he said, 'but I've got to ask it, partly because I believe I shall get a straight answer. There appears to be a general impression that George murdered Mark and subsequently committed suicide. That impression is shared by Lisa and Christopher, who are both highly intelligent people, and I think by Mason, who is certainly no fool. But I don't share it. I find it difficult to believe that George was either a murderer or a suicide, and I don't think I have any illusions about his being a fine character. Now, I don't believe my mind is affected by my visit to China, but I'm perfectly aware that my nerves are. Do you believe that I'm letting my imagination run away with me?'

'Possibly,' said Johnny. 'But if you are, so am I.'

'And so am I,' said Sally.

Richard seemed to relax a little. 'May I have your reasons?' he asked.

'I don't know that I've got any real reasons,' said Johnny. 'I've got one argument, perhaps not very sound, and a collection of hunches. I'll start with the argument. The case for the prosecution is that George came down in the Rover, arrived after you had left — which is perfectly possible if he stopped for lunch en route — entered the house unannounced, found your uncle alone in the study, quarrelled with him, and killed him. Now, I agree that George almost certainly came down here, because it's very difficult to explain the Rover on any other assumption. But I submit that the last thing he would do would be to wander into the house unannounced. I think it's clear that he had no motive for premeditated murder, and really no motive for seeing your uncle at all. Therefore he came, as he said he meant to do, to see you. The last thing he would want to do would be to talk to you in your uncle's presence, and if he wandered into the house, he would almost certainly find you with your uncle. I'm quite aware that there's a counter argument here. George drank, and if George had got tight on the way down, there's no saying what he mightn't have done. But he was a hardened drinker, and I think it would probably have taken more alcohol than he could afford just then to get the better of his natural caution. Would you agree?'

'Yes,' said Richard. 'George could get offensive on comparatively little alcohol — or no alcohol at all. But it took a lot of soaking to put him right off his stroke. He must have had a hell of a party — no doubt at someone else's expense — the night he had that row with Mark, for instance. What's more, he may have been drinking deliberately then, to whip up his courage. He wouldn't have the same reason for priming himself to see me, and a gin or two before lunch certainly wouldn't upset his plans.'

Johnny nodded. 'Then I don't think he wandered into the house. He might have rung the bell and asked to see you privately, but we'd have heard about it from Fenton if he had. The only likely alternative that I can see would be to lurk about waiting for you, either in the grounds, in the hope that you'd come out alone, or, more probably, somewhere on the avenue, so that he could stop you when you left. He wouldn't be likely to pick the wrong avenue, so is it possible that he was there and you missed him? You were a bit preoccupied, no doubt.'

'That's putting it mildly, thank you. I was in a filthy temper and driving like hell. I might have taken him by surprise, and if he'd yelled after me, I probably shouldn't have heard him. But if he saw me leave at a quarter to three, why didn't he leave before twenty-five past?'

'Well, we don't know where he'd left the Rover. It may have taken him a little while to get to it. And he might have gone to have a drink — or try to, since it would be out of hours. The landlord of the Arms might be able to enlighten us. In any case, if he saw you go, he'd have no reason to go up to the house. Even if he didn't see you go, the natural thing to do, ultimately, would be to see if your car was still in the courtyard, which he could do from a little distance. And then he'd go home. But by the time the police got on to him he may well have seen the news of your uncle's death, and he may well have thought it politic to say he hadn't been here at all.'

'Yes,' said Richard slowly. 'All this is much more like George, you know, than the case for the prosecution. As long as we assume he wasn't raging tight, caution and cunning were far more in his line than violence. Anything else, Johnny?'

'As far as the murder is concerned, only a lingering doubt — which I think Sally shares — as to whether anyone who had murdered a man could really come back to the scene of his crime and behave as George behaved on Wednesday. Against that we have to put a statement and a suggestion of Christopher's.' He repeated what Christopher had said about George's escape and George's brazenness.

'I think,' said Richard, 'Christopher was being a little unfair. He always disliked George very much. There's probably some truth in what he says about the escape, but I doubt if George ever learnt to be as brazen as all that.'

'All right. Now we come to his own death. There is, of course, a very strong case for suicide. Remorse, if he murdered your uncle. Possibly fear; we don't know what Mason said to him on Wednesday. No job, and he must have realised, after the scene here, that he'd lost any chance he may have imagined he had of being taken back. Probably lack of funds. Quite possibly a final and rather overwhelming realisation that he was a failure. Quite possibly the depressing effects of alcohol and the small hours — Hill told us, you remember, that he had been dead from six to twelve hours, and probably rather nearer six.

'Well, personally I don't think his behaviour on Wednesday was the behaviour of a man who is going to commit suicide, but my opinion isn't worth very much, because the breaking-point might have come quite suddenly, hours after I saw him last. But there are some other points. There is some reason to believe that the land-agency wasn't his last hope. He told Christopher all about a wonderful job he was going to get. I don't suppose for a moment it was wonderful, but there was probably something in it. And Danby's statement is interesting. He says George wasn't tight when he saw him, and he admitted to Mason that he didn't seem unduly depressed.'

'A talk with Wainwright,' said Richard, 'seems more and more desirable.'

'Yes. And again, if George was contemplating suicide, why bother to come back here? I suppose one could argue that he felt it would be fitting to die near the scene of his crime — or, alternatively, in a place where he'd been happy. But I don't find that very convincing. Why not go back to town — I expect the police paid his return fare to Fanchester — and use the gas fire? Or why not the river in or near Fanchester? And then, why bother about a room for the night? He could just have stayed in the pub till closing time if he wanted to wait till after dark. Though I suppose the room could have been a blind. And finally, this. I don't know whether or not the police have found a suicide note. But if I knew they hadn't, that alone would make me gravely doubtful. I won't say I don't think George was a suicidal type — I didn't know him well enough. But I do believe that if he'd committed suicide he'd have wanted his friends to know that he'd done it, and why.'

'I entirely agree with you,' said Richard.

A short silence followed. Then Johnny said: 'You see what this would mean, of course. If George didn't commit suicide, then, unless he went for a moonlight walk and was sufficiently tight to fall into the dam, he was murdered. And he was almost certainly murdered because he knew something about the first murder. It's unlikely that anyone had any other motive for killing him.'

'Unless you count me, after what he'd said to me,' said Richard with a faint smile. 'But in any case, if George is out, I'm the prime suspect again. This simplifies matters, you know. If George knew something about the first murder, he probably knew it because he was down here when it happened. So the Rover is purely coincidental — right out of it — and we start on the ground floor again.'

Sally said quietly: 'How could you have known George was back here?'

Richard smiled at her. 'Well, I didn't,' he said. 'But I suppose he could have rung me up or something.' He looked at Johnny again. 'You knew Mark had been murdered. Did you see any sign on George's body?'

'Nothing definite,' said Johnny. 'I admit I looked rather carefully. But it was very difficult. He'd been bumping gently against the outlet gate, or whatever you call it, for hours. There was, as you saw, a certain amount of bruising about the head and face, and I couldn't tell whether any of the damage had been done before he went into the water. The blow wouldn't have to be very heavy; indeed, it would have not to be. Whoever hit him would have to be very careful not to kill him, because the doctors would be able to tell whether he was really drowned or whether he only fell into the water after he died. But there are several Judo blows which could have been used to knock him out, and at the same time to send him straight over into the water, if he'd been standing on the edge.'

'And any of these blows might be known to the expert who killed Mark — if he was an expert?' Richard spoke so quietly that it took Sally a moment or two to realise that he was almost uncontrollably angry.

'Yes,' said Johnny. 'Quite possibly.'

After another silence Richard went on. 'Well, I'm not going to let George go down to history as a murderer and a suicide if he was neither and I'm not inclined to let the murderer go free if he's still alive. I broached the subject to Christopher last night, and he shied away at once and told me very firmly not to stick my neck out. So he's no good. And I don't somehow fancy a private detective. I would go out and detect myself, but for one thing, the Press might make it a little difficult, and for another, I'm not quite sure how much more I can take at the moment. I shouldn't do any good if I cracked up, and if my nerves broke down properly it would prejudice any case I might be able to bring. I know it's a hell of a thing to ask, and probably the last thing you want to do, but would you take it on?'

'Have you been reading the papers today?' asked Johnny.

Sally hadn't, and she didn't understand. But Richard said: 'Yes. I'm very sorry the Press has raked up the story. It must be extremely embarrassing for you and your firm, and probably rather painful. But it does suggest that you are good at detective work. If the Press is right, you two found the murderer after the police had arrested the wrong man.'

'That is literally true. But it wasn't as clever as it

sounds. There was a good deal of luck about it. And we were in an extremely favourable position for investigating. We knew nearly everyone concerned very well indeed, and we were able to question anyone we wanted to. We couldn't do that here. I take it you would authorise us to question the servants and put in a word for us with Wainwright and any of the other local people. But we couldn't, for instance, question other people's servants about their masters, and we could hardly put leading questions to any of the suspects. Apart from the ordinary conventions, we'd have to consider the reputation of Heldar's. And even if we weren't hampered in that way, I doubt very much if we should be successful.'

'I can't argue with you,' said Richard, 'and I certainly shouldn't ask you to go beyond decent limits. But even if you think it's a poor chance, I'm still asking you to take it on.'

Johnny was silent for a moment. Then he said: 'There's another thing you'd have to face. If it wasn't George who murdered your uncle, it was probably still someone you know, and possibly a friend of yours.'

'George was a friend of mine,' said Richard.

'Yes. That answers that. It's also possible that some dirty linen might have to be washed. It would at least be washed in private. But if it belonged to your friends, the washing might be embarrassing for you — or conceivably painful.'

'I'll take a chance on that.'

'Very well. Now, Sally. Do we investigate this, or do I investigate it, or do you want notice of the question?'

Sally didn't want to investigate the crimes. She certainly didn't want Johnny to investigate them without her. But she saw Mark smiling at her with amusement and affection, and George, with something piteous now about his brazenness, almost as clearly as she saw

Richard's white face, and realised that for him this moment was one of almost intolerable strain. He got up suddenly and said: 'Please forgive me. You both want to sleep on this.'

'No, indeed we don't,' she said. 'Of course we investigate it.'

CHAPTER SEVEN

After breakfast the next morning Richard rang up the landlord of the Thaxton Arms, ascertained from him that all the reporters had gone back to town for the moment, and discreetly commended the Heldars to his good offices. They were therefore well received when they reached the Arms twenty minutes later by way of the short cut through the park.

Wainwright took them into a small private sitting room at the back of the house.

'Now,' he said. 'I don't know what you want of me, but Mr Richard says I'm to give it you, an' that's good enough. So go ahead, please, sir.'

Richard had told them that Wainwright was an intelligent man, and unlikely to gossip about anything which seriously concerned the manor and had advised them to be fairly frank with him. Johnny told him briefly what they were trying to do, and he looked sharply at them and said: 'That's interestin', that is. I was surprised at Mr Willesdon committin' suicide. But there was plenty of talk about 'im murderin' Sir Mark — the police were askin' the 'ole village if they'd seen 'im on the day of the murder — so I took it 'e'd done it out of remorse, like. But if there's any serious doubt about 'im killin' the old gentleman, that puts a different face on it, sir. I wouldn't say 'e was like a man that was goin' to jump in the river.'

'Would you tell us about that evening he was here — all about it?'

'Surely, sir. 'E got off the bus outside 'ere at a quarter to eight — two of my customers saw 'im — an' 'e walked in an' asked for supper an' a bed, as cool as you like. I wasn't too keen, for more reasons than one. If you'll excuse plain speakin', sir, 'e could get very nasty when 'e'd 'ad a drink or two — not violent, but very rude — an' 'e made trouble in the bar parlour more than once when 'e was livin' 'ere. An' I didn't know if I'd get paid, either, for I've known 'im order drinks when 'e 'adn't the money to pay for them. Then again, 'alf the village thought 'e was a murderer, an' I wasn't too sure of 'im myself. But I couldn't refuse 'im, for 'e showed me two five-pound notes.'

'You're quite sure of that?' asked Johnny, a little startled.

'Quite sure, sir. 'E pulled 'em 'alf out of 'is wallet an' said: "You can't chuck me out, Wainwright, not unless I get tight. An' I'm not goin' to get tight tonight!"'

'Really? That's interesting.'

'I didn't believe it, sir. I just didn't believe that Mr Willesdon, with ten pounds in 'is pocket, would be able to stay sober all evenin' in a pub. But 'e did. 'E 'ad 'is supper — some cold rabbit pie an' cheese an' a bottle o' beer — an' then 'e went into the bar parlour an' 'e 'ad two gins — which, of course, was nothin' to 'im. No one was very keen to talk to 'im, an' 'e got some old-fashioned looks, but 'e didn't seem to mind. 'E just sat in a corner by 'imself until the Colonel came in. That was about twenty to nine. The Colonel doesn't often come in, but 'e'd been for a stroll, an' it was a warm evenin', an' 'e wanted a glass o' beer.

'Well, 'e took one look at Mr Willesdon, an' 'e says: "What, are you still 'ere?" "Yes," says Mr Willesdon. "Any objection?" The Colonel looked at 'im for a minute, an' I kept an eye on 'em, because—' Wainwright stopped. 'Maybe I'm lettin' my tongue run away with me, sir. You'll 'ave 'eard all this from the Colonel 'imself.'

'More or less,' said Johnny. 'But please go on. The Colonel's a bit quick-tempered, isn't he?'

'Well, yes, sir. An' 'e was never on very good terms with Mr Willesdon. 'E didn't approve of Mr Willesdon's 'abits, an' 'e didn't think 'e knew 'is job. Anyway, after a minute 'e said: "I've no personal objection, but I wonder you 'ad the face to come back 'ere at all," an' 'e got very red. Mr Willesdon said: "Be careful, old boy. Bad for the blood pressure," an' I thought the Colonel was goin' to lose 'is temper good an' proper. But Mr Willesdon said somethin' to 'im quiet, an' 'e seemed to take an 'old on 'imself, though I saw 'im clench 'is fists. They talked for a minute or two, still quiet — I didn't 'ear a word — an' then the Colonel turned an' walked out. An' Mr Willesdon picked up 'is glass o' beer that 'e'd left, an' drank it, an' 'e was smilin'. After that 'e sat quiet in 'is corner again, lookin' at a paper someone brought in, but 'e didn't look as if 'is mind was on it. 'E looked as if 'e was thinkin' about somethin' else, an' every now an' then 'e'd smile to 'imself again.'

'He was happy, then?'

'In a quiet way, sir. In a kind of a secret way, too, I'd say. I didn't quite like the look of 'im, to tell you the truth. In fact — if you'll excuse me, ma'am — I just 'oped it wasn't a girl 'e 'ad on 'is mind. There was a nasty business when 'e was at Westwater, with one of the local girls. I never knew all the rights of it, an' she was a silly little fool anyway, but 'e didn't be'ave as 'e should 'ave. Well, anyway, 'e sat there till closing time, an' never 'ad another drink, an' when everyone 'ad gone 'e went up to bed. 'E 'adn't any luggage with 'im, an' I remarked on that when 'e said good night, but 'e said it wouldn't matter for tonight. Not "for one night", you understand, but "for tonight". Which, of course, might be taken to mean that 'e was plannin' to end it that night.

'I never saw 'im again, an' I didn't 'ear 'im go out in the night, an' nor did anyone else. But when I got up in the mornin' the front door was unbolted, an' I wondered. 'E was the only guest in the 'ouse, so I went up to 'is room to 'ave a look. 'E wasn't there, nor any of 'is things. 'E'd been lyin' on the bed, but 'e 'adn't got into it. Well, thinks I, either 'e's skipped, or there was a girl in it. Then 'e didn't turn up for breakfast, so I took it 'e'd skipped. An' that was all, until the police arrived.'

'Tell me,' said Johnny, 'do you know if he left any sort of suicide note?'

'I never saw one, sir. I didn't search 'is room, of course, an' the police did. But you'd think if 'e was goin' to leave one 'e'd leave it where it would be easy to see.'

'You would. Now, one more question, which the police must already have asked you. Did you see Willesdon on the day of Sir Mark's death?'

'No,' said Wainwright. 'An' I 'aven't 'eard of anyone else that actually saw 'im that day. But there's a man 'oo says 'e saw Mr Richard's old Rover, an' there seems to be some idea that Mr Willesdon was drivin' it that day.'

'When and where did he see it?' asked Johnny.

'Well, sir, you know the road on the west side of the park, an' the lane that goes off to Sir Mark's farm an' the dam? Yes. Well, this chap — 'is name's Bill Slater, an' 'e lives up 'Orse Lane, the other side o' the road, an' keeps pigs. 'E was walkin' along the road — goin' south, with 'is back to the west gate — somewhere between a quarter past two an' 'alf past. Mr Richard's Rover overtook 'im an' turned into the farm lane. 'E didn't see 'oo was in it, so 'e took it to be Mr Richard. 'E didn't turn down the lane, an' 'e didn't see it again. But 'e'll tell you 'imself, sir, if you ask 'im.'

Wainwright insisted on entertaining them before they left and brought in three bottles of beer. Johnny was obliged to close the proceedings with a short business talk, for Richard had insisted that the Arms shouldn't lose by its hospitality to George. Wainwright shook his head and said quietly and firmly that Mr Richard was a real genuine Thaxton, but that was no reason why he should lose by it either.

* * *

THEY DIDN'T GO STRAIGHT BACK to Westwater. They bought cigarettes at the village shop, where they were well received and looked at with interest, and then Johnny said quietly: 'Would you mind very much if we walked from here to the dam?'

'No, I wouldn't mind, darling.'

They walked on to the old stone bridge, skirted a row of cottages, and found a path running by the riverside. The river was obviously a smallish affair at the best of times, and the long drought had made it shallow; it wouldn't, as Johnny pointed out, have been an entirely satisfactory means of either suicide or murder by drowning, which was presumably why the dam had been chosen.

'And because it made a definite rendezvous, I suppose,' said Sally. 'But how did the murderer persuade George to come?'

'There's probably a rather unpleasant answer to that. I should think George was blackmailing him. Then he could say: "I'll meet you at the dam at two in the morning and give you the money." Do you remember George's pretty little trick after the inquest, Sally? "If you don't let me come back to tea I'll talk to the Press." It came very pat — too pat. I'll swear George was a natural blackmailer in little things like that. I wouldn't be surprised if he tried it on in a big thing if he got the chance.'

'Could he have been blackmailing Danby in the pub?'

'It's possible, though he hadn't much time for it. Danby could have shut him up quickly because it was a public place but agreed to meet him and discuss it later. George might have objected to leaving his comfortable bed, but if Danby had already decided to kill him, he might have made some excuse to get him out. It was after that, you remember, that Wainwright noticed George smiling to himself, and that George said his being short of pyjamas didn't matter for tonight. On the other hand, it was before that that he decided to keep sober.'

'Yes,' said Sally, 'and if he came back with the intention of blackmailing Danby, why did he wait? Wainwright said Danby didn't often come to the pub, so George wouldn't have been expecting him. Why didn't he go and call on him?'

'Possibly he intended to, later in the evening. Or possibly Danby's domestic circumstances made a call undesirable — though he's unmarried and I think he lives alone. I've no doubt Mason's been into all this. Danby didn't admit the quarrel when he was questioned at the dam, but Mason must have got the story from Wainwright — which probably explains why he questioned Danby again at lunchtime. But look at it this way, Sally. Any one of the known suspects *might* have invented a reason for dragging George out of bed and bringing him to the dam. But a much more plausible reason could be given by someone who quite ob-

best of his recollection the ex-batman slept above the kitchen, in a room reached by a separate staircase, and that Danby could probably have left the house to meet George at the dam without the man's hearing him.

The question of the Rover's tyres was referred to Lisa, who was unable to help, except for a vague idea that they had been old when she had last used the car, nearly three years ago. She had never had a new one fitted. Sally was inclined to be sympathetic; she was almost entirely vague about tyres herself.

'There's one slightly curious point,' said Richard when Johnny had finished. 'Why did George go to so much trouble to hide the car? It was scarcely necessary if he only wanted to come and intercept me. And even if he did kill Mark, we're agreed that the murder wasn't premeditated.'

Lisa shrugged her shoulders. 'He would not wish Mark to hear that he had been at Westwater, and the Rover, with its distinctive number, was well known in the neighbourhood. You or I, perhaps, would not have taken so much trouble, but George had a tortuous mind.'

'True,' said Richard. 'Well, what do you want to do next, Johnny?'

'I'd like to see Bill Slater. I'd also like to talk to the gardeners and the lodge-keepers. Not with any very definite end in view, but just in case something turns up.'

'Certainly. I'll come and recommend you. There's just one thing, though. There's no one in the west lodge just now — at least, not officially. Mark told me on Monday afternoon that he was having various repairs and renovations done there, and an old couple called Jakes were moving into it when it was ready. Apparently Jakes has been doing some of the odd jobs himself, and he may or may not have been there on

Monday afternoon. All of which, of course, would have given me a reasonable motive for leaving by the west avenue if I hadn't wanted my time of departure noted. But we can see Jakes at his cottage if he's not at the lodge.'

The interrogation of the gardeners was not very fruitful. On the afternoon of the murder the head gardener and the gardener's boy had been working together on the east side of the house, and at some distance from it. Except when they had gone into the kitchen for tea, they had seen no one but each other. They had seen no car, and neither could remember having heard one. Betts was a little more informative. He had been working near the west avenue, but out of sight of it. He had seen Christopher in the early part of the afternoon, and exchanged a few words with him, but couldn't say at what time; it might have been about half-past two. Later he had heard a car come up the west avenue, and from the way its brakes had been handled had identified it as the Colonel's. Unfortunately he was again vague about the time; it had been before he went in for his tea at four, but how long before he couldn't remember.

After lunch they collected Johnny's car from the stables and took the opportunity of questioning the chauffeur. But Morley had spent Monday afternoon in the garage, and except in his tea interval had seen no one; nor had he heard or seen any car outside. They drove down to the north lodge and sat in the hot little kitchen with the old woman who kept it. But Mrs Thorne hadn't seen George or anyone else of interest on Monday afternoon, and she hadn't seen the Rover. What was rather disturbing was that she hadn't seen or heard Richard leave. She had gone into the village at about half-past two, had called on a friend, and hadn't got home till about four.

There was no one to be seen at the west lodge, and Richard said they had better take Bill Slater next, and guided Johnny a little way down the road and up Horse Lane. They found Slater among his pigs. He greeted Richard warmly, and then leaned on the door of a sty and talked. There seemed to be no doubt that he had seen the Rover; he described it in detail and gave the number. He had already told Mason about it — but only, they gathered, when he had been sure that Richard hadn't been in it.

They drove on up the lane, which almost at once curved to the left and ran into another. This, said Richard, was Jakes' lane, which came out on the road a couple of hundred yards to the south of the west gate. They stopped outside a tumbledown cottage at which he looked with disfavour. 'I don't wonder Mark wanted to get them out of here,' he said. 'It's gone down badly while I've been away.'

The Jakeses hadn't met him since his return, and their welcome was touching. The old woman cried a little, and Richard forgot his careful restraint and put an arm round her. Then he presented Lisa, and Mrs Jakes reverted to her youth and bobbed a curtsey. It was some time before they got down to questioning.

Jakes spoke the Hampshire of his fathers, but his evidence was clear enough. No, he hadn't seen Mr Willesdon — of whom he had obviously disapproved — on the day Sir Mark had been killed. He hadn't seen anyone about Westwater, except young Frankie Pearce — the gardener's boy — on his way home from work, and the Colonel.

'When did you see the Colonel?' asked Johnny.

The question was settled — more or less — after some reference to the grandfather clock which had belonged to Mrs Jakes' uncle, and a good deal of discussion about what Mrs Jakes had said to Jakes, and he to her, before he left for the west lodge to do a job of carpentry. That had probably been about twenty past three, or a minute or two after.

'Oi come round the last bend in the lane, an' Oi see the Colonel's car goin' past in the road. 'E started to blow 'is 'orn — always makes more noise than anyone else, the Colonel does. Oi never drove a car, but Oi'd 'old 'er in at lodge gates rather than make a noise you'd 'ear in Fanchester. When Oi come to the gate 'e was just passin' out o' sight up the avenue.'

'You didn't see any other car on the road?' asked Johnny.

'No, Oi didn't, sir.'

'Did you see Mr Richard's old car at any time that day?'

'The old black one, wi' three threes on 'er? No, sir.'

As they drove away Johnny said: 'This doesn't prove that the Rover was there, but it does suggest that Danby was speaking the truth about that. If Jakes had just come round this bend when he saw the Colonel, the Rover had presumably already passed the foot of the lane — if it was coming from the waterman's cottage. And Betts's evidence suggests that it was never on the west avenue.'

"Old 'er in at lodge gates,' said Richard. 'Yes, it does.'

'What I don't quite like is that Jakes saw Danby's car passing out of sight on the avenue. That first bend is a fair way up. Wouldn't it have been quicker, if he was going to the farm, to start walking from a little way above the lodge?'

'A little, but there's not much in it.'

'Well, there's not and there may be. The time factor is pretty close.' Johnny drew up just out of sight of the lodge. 'Suppose he stopped here. It was just before half-past three. He'd have to get to the farm, have a glance round, get back here, drive on to the house, and be in the study at a quarter to four. He's an elderly man, and it was a hot afternoon. I'm sorry, but I think we ought to try it out. Will you come with me? You know the shortest way from this point.'

Richard led them at a fast walk across the park. The farm was a good deal nearer to their starting point than to the house, but it took them seven minutes to reach it. Johnny gave them one minute by his watch before starting back. When they reached the car he drove fast, and they got quickly out and hurried up to the terrace and into the quiet study.

'Not quite eighteen minutes,' he said. 'Yes. I suppose we could allow him up to nineteen, or even twenty. Neither he nor Jakes is certain to a minute what time he reached the gate. It is possible, though a little tight.'

'He always walks fast when he's excited,' said Richard.

After that Johnny asked his permission to question the servants, but the results were unhelpful. None of the servants had seen George or the Rover on the afternoon of the murder. None of them had heard anyone moving in or outside the house on the night of George's death. Deane, questioned afterwards, gave the same answers, and added that on Monday afternoon he had heard a car on the west avenue — probably the Colonel's, from the squealing of its brakes — but couldn't say at what time, except that it had been after his visit to the door of the study. He had heard no other car. Gloria, questioned further, admitted with a touching relief that she hadn't actually seen Deane go into the study. Mason had interrogated her again on that point, and she had realised that she might well have been wrong.

Back in the library, Johnny took out his scheme of evidence.

'One or two points need amendment,' he said, 'in the

light of increased knowledge. In view of Jakes' evidence and Deane's, it almost certainly wasn't Danby to whom Mercator was talking at three-five. He may have paid two separate visits to the study, but it seems most unlikely. He almost certainly didn't arrive before about three-thirty, and by that time, surely, Mercator would have fetched Christopher if he'd been alive. Danby could have got to the farm and back before three-forty-five. So he probably didn't do the murder. The medical evidence, of course, doesn't let anyone out. The doctors simply said that Mercator could have been killed at any time between two-twenty, when we all saw him alive, and approximately three-forty-five, when we found him dead.'

'And they said he could have been killed by the blow you described.'

Johnny nodded. 'But of course,' he said, 'the principal difference is that, as Richard pointed out last night, we no longer have to fit in the Rover.'

'So it could really have been anyone.'

'Yes. It could really have been anyone.'

134

CHAPTER EIGHT

Sunday was an uncomfortable day, principally, from Sally's point of view, because she knew that Johnny was very worried. They finished sorting out the libraries, but Johnny was absent-minded, and the work went slowly. He was reluctant to discuss the murder question, even with her, and she didn't bother him about it. But by the end of the day she was almost certain that it wasn't the murder question alone that was worrying him — or, at any rate, it was some aspect of the question that she herself couldn't see.

The inquest on George was held on Monday afternoon; Christopher came down as a witness. They ran the gauntlet of the Press again and listened to evidence in the stuffy public bar. But the result was a foregone conclusion. The medical witnesses seemed perfectly satisfied that George had drowned himself. Richard, Wainwright, and Johnny did what they could to suggest that in their opinion George's state of mind had not been suicidal. But it seemed that the Coroner didn't agree with them, and the jury didn't agree with them either. A verdict of suicide was brought in, and the foreman added that, in the jury's opinion, Mr

Willesdon had done it out of remorse, because he had murdered Sir Mark Mercator. The jury was severely reprimanded for this rider but seemed to feel that it had done its duty.

Richard made it quite clear, when they returned to Westwater, that he was dissatisfied with the verdict, and since no one was inclined to deceive Christopher, he discovered without difficulty that private enquiries were being made. He disapproved strongly, and was only partially pacified, after a long and trying argument, by Johnny's assurance that the enquiries would be kept within the bounds of decency.

It was Lisa who in the course of the argument, by a mixture of charm and lack of inhibition, managed to get a little information out of him. He denied that George had said anything to him about coming back to Danesfield, and it was then that Lisa asked him — gently and very reasonably — if he had given George two five-pound notes. He flushed crimson and admitted that he had.

'He told me he was down to his last few shillings. Whether it was true or not I wouldn't like to say. But when I said there was nothing doing, he indicated that he would try to borrow from Richard, and I didn't want him coming back here or writing begging letters.'

'Thank you, Christopher,' said Lisa, and smiled at him. But Sally thought she saw the reason for this unexpected assistance. Lisa believed that George was guilty, or even if she wasn't sure of it, she didn't want the matter investigated, because as long as the police believed in George's guilt Richard was safe. But she didn't really believe that any investigations could clear George, and she was demonstrating that — showing Johnny and Richard that they were up against a blank wall. The sooner they realised that, the sooner they would give up.

The Heldars went up to town next morning. Lisa had provided them with a key to the lock-up in the mews and a set of keys for the Rover, and at lunchtime they drove out to look at the car. It seemed likely that the police had been interested in it — in which case they had probably borrowed George's keys — but they had either left it here or brought it back. It stood, old and rather battered and a little dusty, under the harsh electric light.

Johnny examined the tyres and said: 'Yes. A Dunlop, not very new...an old Firestone...two more very old Dunlops. And a patch of oil on the floor. Well, I'm satisfied now that this car was left at the waterman's cottage, but that doesn't get us much further.'

They looked inside the car but found nothing of interest. Then Johnny drove back to the shop, and Sally took his car on, bought something for supper, and went home. She had had a feeling that Johnny wanted to get away from Westwater for as long as possible, and when she had suggested making an excuse for not going back to dinner, he had jumped at it.

He came in late, for he had had a good deal of work to make up, looking tired and anxious. Sally gave him a drink and fed him and kept off the subject of Westwater until they were back in the sitting room, drinking their coffee. Then she said: 'Darling, would you like to come clean? Not unless you want to, of course.'

Johnny looked at his watch. 'Quarter to eight,' he said. 'We ought to leave at half-past at the latest. Yes, I would like to come clean. It seems easier to do it when we're not under Richard's roof — though that's probably rather ridiculous.'

'Richard?'

'Darling, don't you see? If we count George out, we

can bring a water-tight case against Richard, and we can't bring one against anyone else.'

Sally stared at him. 'Of course there always was a case against Richard,' she said. 'But surely that's dead now. Richard would never have asked us to investigate if he'd done the murder — or murders — himself. He'd have shared the general impression of George's guilt.'

'I know, Sally. There may be an argument against that — I'm not sure. The point at the moment is that Richard has asked us to prove George's innocence, and I've been splitting my head over the problem all this last weekend, and the only way I can do it is to prove Richard himself guilty.'

Sally waited, and after a moment he went slowly on.

'Deane is still in the running, of course. But he's such a poor actor that I simply cannot believe he isn't telling the truth now. Besides, there isn't the faintest suggestion that he knew George had come back on Wednesday evening. Danby is still just possible. But the time factor is very much against his having murdered Mark. I don't think he had time to arrange the rendezvous with George when they met at the pub — George would almost certainly have argued the question. The words which Wainwright didn't hear may have been an unpleasant Georgian reminder of Danby's head wound. Anyhow, I'm sure the rendezvous was arranged before George arrived at the pub — otherwise, why would he have bothered to keep sober? It's still possible that the murder was committed by one of the servants, or by someone we've never even thought of or perhaps even heard of. But I find it extremely difficult to suspect any of the servants, and even the police, with all their facilities for investigation, don't seem to have dug up any evidence of mysterious strangers about the place.

'Well, that leaves us with Richard and Christopher.

It boils down to a simple and straightforward argument. Either Mark never fetched Christopher because Richard killed him before he could do so, or he did fetch Christopher and Christopher killed him.

'As far as opportunity is concerned, there's nothing to choose between them. But look at the question of motive. Richard had an excellent motive for unpremeditated murder, particularly in view of his nervous condition. That will would have made anyone see red. And I can't quite accept the motive which Lisa has attributed to Christopher. The more I see and hear of him, the less I can believe that he would resort to violence, even under the provocation she suggested. His temperament — his background — his record — they all seem to weigh heavily against it.

'There's another motive we have to consider: the motive for abstracting and then concealing the will. Now I just can't accept the motive Lisa has ascribed to Christopher — in Christopher's case. On the other hand, Richard would have had much the same motive — except that it would have been entirely personal and not partially vicarious — and no professional inhibitions about yielding to it. He may have had some idea that the clause in restraint of marriage could be set aside, and he evidently knew he didn't benefit under the previous will.'

'Yes,' said Sally, 'but he'd have to have professional advice on that. He didn't hear Christopher's opinion till the next morning, and he told Mason about the will that same evening. That would have been a mad thing to do if he was still thinking of suppressing it. It would have been unwise even if he'd already decided to let it be found; he'd have saved himself a lot of trouble by pretending he'd never seen it.'

'I know, darling. But we've got to remember that he was in an abnormal nervous condition — he ended up by fainting, you know. He may very well have said things he didn't mean to. He may even have fainted because he realised he was slipping. I don't suggest he actually staged the faint — I doubt if Mason would have been taken in — but there is such a thing as letting oneself go. He may even have learnt the technique in his prison camp; it's one way of stopping the torture for the time being. But to return to the will. Supposing Lisa suspected from the first that Richard was the murderer — she's highly intelligent, as he said himself, and she seems to know him pretty well. She observed his interest in the possibility of setting aside the restraining clause — you remember she said the will was almost the only thing he would talk to Christopher about — and she guessed that he had abstracted it, and why. And then, by a rather bold stroke, she attributed his motive to Christopher. I don't suppose she really wanted Christopher charged with murder; she just wanted to confuse the issue, and she hoped her story would go from you to me and from me to Mason.'

'Perhaps,' said Sally unhappily, 'she didn't only suspect Richard.'

'Yes, he might have told her. But not at all necessarily.' Johnny lit another cigarette, and then went on.

'Now we come to George's death. Christopher could have known George was coming back. But I don't think George would have agreed to come back just to suit Christopher, and I'm inclined to accept Christopher's explanation of the ten pounds, with only the reservation that he made the donation with a view even more to sparing Lisa than to sparing Richard. But Richard took a telephone call from Fanchester on Wednesday evening. The caller was apparently reluctant to give his name to Fenton, but said he was a member of Richard's old squadron — a sure draw for Richard. Richard said afterwards that he was a reporter, and an impertinent call from a reporter might have made him look as grim as he did. But a blackmailing call from George certainly would. And the call came through before seven, so George wouldn't have been on the bus.'

'It is water-tight,' said Sally after a while. 'But would Richard have asked us to investigate if he'd done it? You said there might be an argument against that.'

'It's very difficult to find a good one. But one might argue something like this. It has been generally assumed by the Westwater neighbourhood that George murdered Mark and committed suicide. But there will be no trial and no conviction. The world at large — and possibly some of Richard's own friends — won't hear that George did it and may suspect Richard; it did come out at the inquest that he quarrelled with Mark. But if it were to become known, at any rate among his friends, that he didn't believe George was guilty, and actually set private investigations on foot to disprove it — well, that would weigh quite heavily in his favour. He believes himself safe, because he doesn't think George's guilt can be disproved — at any rate by a couple of amateurs — and in any case the mere fact that he's asked us to investigate should prevent us from suspecting him. One might even argue that if he'd really wanted George proved innocent, he'd have gone to a professional.'

'Do you really believe this?' asked Sally.

'I don't think so,' said Johnny. 'I'm just rather unhappy about it. If we can't do any better in the next few days, I'm afraid we shall have to report failure and withdraw.'

* * *

THEY REACHED Westwater just after ten, took the car straight to the stables, and walked through the garden to the terrace. As they approached the lighted windows of the drawing room they raised their voices tactfully. But the effort was wasted, for they heard a man's voice which wasn't Richard's.

He was a plump, elderly man with a round, cheerful face, and he was talking to Lisa and Richard, with a tumbler of whisky at his elbow. Lisa saw the Heldars first and jumped up. To Sally's astonishment her face was happy.

'Johnny!' she said. 'Richard is cleared! Mr Glover saw him drive out of the north gate just after a quarter to three.'

'We asked him to stay and tell you about it himself,' said Richard. He made introductions and got the Heldars drinks. Then he looked at Mr Glover, and Mr Glover smiled and nodded.

'Well,' he said, 'I'd better give it to you properly. My name is James Glover; I'm an accountant with an office in Fanchester — Carsway and Glover and I live at Rosewood Cottage, Danesfield. On the afternoon poor Sir Mark was killed I was driving into Fanchester. It was the first day of my summer holiday. I had to meet my daughter and her family; they were coming to us for one night, and then we were all going to Shanklin for a week. As I was meeting a train, I was keeping an eye on the time — and so was my wife. We're both quite sure it was nearly two-forty-five when I left the house — the train is due at three-twenty. So it must have been just after two-forty-five when I came to the north gate of Westwater. Just as I slowed down, a last year's Armstrong Siddeley Sapphire came out, with Richard driving. I've known Richard all his life, and I couldn't possibly have mistaken anyone else for him. I waved to him, but he didn't see me. He was going very fast. Too fast for safety.' Glover smiled again. 'I was glad I'd slowed down. He turned right — presumably for London — and passed round the bend and out of my ken. I didn't see him again. But I gather I saw enough of him to give him an alibi. If I'd had any idea it was important, I'd have come forward long before now. But being on the beach at Shanklin, I didn't hear the local news. We got back this afternoon, and this evening, when I was in my garden, young Betts from the manor came along and stopped for a chat. I'm afraid I'm a bit of a gossip — or so my wife always tells me — and I listened to what he had to say about the murder. Presently it began to dawn on me that Richard's time of departure was rather important. So I checked my own time of departure with my wife and came up to tell him about it. I shall go and tell Inspector Mason first thing tomorrow morning.'

After that Mr Glover went away. But an hour later Johnny said out of the darkness: 'This is grand, of course. Absolutely grand. But if neither George nor Richard did the murder, who the hell did?'

'I wouldn't know,' said Sally drowsily. 'And at the moment, I wouldn't very much care.'

* * *

THEY WENT to London again the next day, and Sally tried to make up some more arrears of housework. She was still anxious. Now that Richard's innocence was proved beyond doubt, she was very much afraid that they had been wrong, and that George was guilty after all. No other explanation seemed reasonable. And if Richard had to accept George's guilt, it would be a bad blow for him. But at least he was out of it himself, and that was an enormous relief. It was curious how much she and Johnny had come to like Richard, in such a short time.

Johnny had said he would be home for lunch about a quarter to one. He walked in at half-past twelve, and as soon as she saw him Sally knew that something was badly wrong. When he had kissed her, he said quietly: 'I'm afraid I've got some perfectly horrible news, darling. Lisa has just rung me up to say that Mason has arrested Richard.'

'Arrested *Richard?* But hasn't he heard Glover's evidence?'

'I'm very much afraid Glover's evidence may have helped to arrest Richard. Mason told Lisa one or two things — I gather she bombarded him with questions. But there isn't time to go into details now. She wanted us to come down, and I said we would — at least, I said I would. But I must see Mason on the way. I can at least tell him Richard asked us to investigate, though I dare say Lisa's told him that already. How soon can we lunch, darling?'

'Now. It's cold.'

They started before one o'clock, letting the washing-up go. Johnny didn't talk until they had left the traffic behind.

Then he said slowly: 'You remember that when I worked out that scheme, I said that one might make out a case against Richard on the assumption that he used both the Armstrong and the Rover. I didn't take it very seriously at the time, partly because it involved an accomplice, but chiefly because it seemed to break down on Christopher's presence. Richard knew Mark was going to fetch Christopher as soon as he'd gone, so he couldn't have hoped to come back and kill Mark a little later on. Well, I've seen a possible answer to that now, and I think Mason must have seen one too. Because, according to Lisa, he's arrested Richard for committing the murder with George as an accomplice.'

'George? You suggested Lisa in the scheme.'

'I know. I thought at that time that the Rover would probably have been used to incriminate George. But in view of the evidence we've heard since, Mason's idea is certainly sounder. I think he's probably worked it out something like this.' Johnny paused to collect his thoughts, and then went on.

'Richard and George together laid a plan of murder. Richard was obviously the brains of the concern, and George was probably persuaded to co-operate by the promise of the land-agency, or a sum of money, or both. Because of Christopher's presence the plan had to be altered a bit at short notice, but it was carried out substantially as it was laid.

'At eleven-forty-five or thereabouts, Richard left Lisa's flat in the Armstrong. Just after that George rang up Lisa and asked for Richard — to prove that he had no idea Richard was going to Westwater, and that therefore there was no collusion between them. At twelve-fifteen or thereabouts — evidence of the publisher type — George left the mews in the Rover. At one-thirty or a little after, Richard arrived at Westwater — and found Christopher there. He realised at once that Christopher's presence would probably throw his whole plan out. You remember how violently he re-acted, and it may not have been only because he knew Christopher was in love with Lisa — though I don't suppose anyone has told Mason about that. But he probably decided to wait and see how things turned out. It would still have been perfectly possible to call the murder off for that day. In fact, I imagine he was going to give Mark a last chance to agree to his mar-rying Lisa and kill him only if he still refused. But that depends on his motive for premeditated murder, which is still a little uncertain.

'In any case, between two-fifteen and two-thirty — evidence of Bill Slater — George arrived at the waterman's cottage. They allowed two and a half hours for his trip — a little more, because I don't think Richard could have met him till about five to three — but that's reasonable enough, because the Rover's an old car.

'Now, I think Richard intended from the first to leave Westwater at about a quarter to three. It would be about the earliest moment at which he reasonably could leave, and he wanted all his time, because he had to come back again by way of the terrace, which might involve dodging the gardeners, kill Mark and get away again before, let us say, a quarter or ten to four. Soon after that Fenton would come to the study to announce tea, and from then on, we might be with Mark. But I'm pretty certain that, before he left, Richard was going to make sure of his alibi. Perhaps he was going to say goodbye to us and try to make us see him off. He would also, of course, hope to be seen by Mrs Thorne at the north gate. The best thing would have been to arrange — in addition to all that — for someone to see Mark alive within the next twenty minutes or so. That would have been ticklish, and the witness might have stayed a little too long for Richard's convenience, but he expected to have a little time to play about with.

'But in the meantime Mark sprang the will on him. He was extremely angry but didn't do violence at once. He must have realised that Mark had brought Christopher down to give him the will, and my guess is that that suggested a means of keeping Christopher out of the study long enough for his purpose. I think he begged Mark earnestly to reconsider the will, quietly and by himself, for, say, half an hour. If by the end of that time he hadn't changed his mind, then he could

146

fetch Christopher and give it to him. I think Mark might well have agreed to that, and if he did, Richard would know he'd keep his word. He might have asked Mark to think it over till tea time, which would have given him more time, but Mark might have refused that. Anyway, I'm inclined to think time was tight, because Richard went away without making any attempt to consolidate his alibi. He was very shaken, of course, by the will incident, and he may just have lost his head.

'Now according to Glover he turned right at the north gate — presumably for London. He'd have to do that, for the benefit of Mrs Thorne. But you know how the sides of the valley are all seamed with little lanes running up towards the downs. I looked at the estate map the other day, and there's one which runs off that road half a mile east of the north gate, and links up both with Bill Slater's lane and with the one just beyond it, which comes out almost opposite the farm lane. They're tricky driving, of course, and he must have driven fast — as Glover said he was doing. But he knows them inside out, and they'd get him to the farm without touching the village, and almost without touching a road. I say the farm, and not the farm lane, because he'd want to take the car as far as he could, to save time. With luck, I think, he'd be there in ten minutes — at three-fifty-five. And as soon as he got there, George took over the Armstrong and drove like hell for London, getting on to the normal road as soon as he could. He probably wore a hat or a cap, to conceal the fact that he hadn't got red hair, and perhaps sunglasses.

'In the meantime, Richard returned to Westwater on foot, across the park. It took us just over a quarter of an hour from the waterman's cottage, walking at a normal fast pace. Starting from the farm, and really hurrying, I think he could do it in ten minutes. He'd have to go carefully in the grounds, of course, but we know none of the gardeners were between the park gate and the house, or in sight of the terrace. He could have been in the study at five past three. He could have told Mark he'd come back to hear his decision, and Mark could have replied that nothing he could say would alter it. So he killed Mark. It's possible that he meant to do something more about his alibi — and George's: smash Mark's watch, say, so that it stopped at the time of the murder. But either he lost his head again, or he decided that whatever he had meant to do would look too obviously fabricated. He took the will, returned across the park, reached the waterman's cottage at about three-twenty, and left for London in the Rover, being seen by Danby at the west gate at about three-twenty-five.

'After this we enter upon pure speculation. But I think George, when he reached London, must have established an alibi. He told us he'd had tea at a Lyons'. He could probably have got to a suitable one by about a quarter to five, and it would be quite easy to be remembered in a Lyons' if you wanted to be — he could draw himself to the attention of one of the staff, and they're not very full at that time of day. If he were there at four-forty-five, and if Richard had managed to establish the time of the murder at about three-five, then he couldn't have done it — assuming, as the police would almost certainly assume, that he'd been driving the Rover.

'At a guess, I'd say the Lyons' was not too far from Lisa's flat, and he left the Armstrong nearby for Richard to pick up — possibly at some point where he hoped the police would soon find it. If they did, that would strengthen Richard's alibi. I'd say Richard didn't return the Rover to the mews; it would be somewhere about five-thirty when he got back to town — about the time people come home from work — and someone would be very likely to notice him. He could hardly try to pass himself off as George, because the inhabitants of the mews knew George. I think he'd leave the Rover at some prearranged point where the police were not so likely to find it, for George to pick up and put away later on. Then he'd pick up the Armstrong and give a bobby a fair chance to appear and ask why he'd left it there so long. If that happened, he'd say he'd been having a late tea somewhere. If it didn't, he'd fall back on the story of having been delayed by nerves. And assuming the bobby didn't turn up to delay him, he would have reached Lisa's flat, as he says he did, about five-forty-five.'

'It's horribly plausible,' said Sally.

Johnny gave her a quick glance, which came to her as a shock. She was so used to his habit of theorising, for convenience, in the present indicative, that she hadn't realised that now, at last, this was what he really believed to have happened. Perhaps he wasn't dead certain, but he was as certain as made no matter. He had been trying to break it gently. He put a hand on her knee and held it for a moment. Then he went quietly on.

'And the rest is simple. Possibly Richard reckoned without George's blackmailing propensities. Of course George couldn't have given him away without betraying himself. But he may have been getting rather deeper in than they'd expected, and he may have persuaded Richard that he felt his best chance was to turn Queen's Evidence. Or, more likely, there was no question of blackmail, and they merely met — so George at least believed — to discuss a difficult situation. Richard may have decided he would be safer without George, or he may simply have lost his temper in the course of the proceedings — though the circumstances imply premeditation.

'And there's one other thing, Sally. Ever since Mark

was murdered, I've been just a little worried about his accident. I haven't said anything, because I've no evidence at all, and also because it seemed likely that his murder was unpremeditated. If it was, you see, that ruled out a first attempt. But supposing someone pulled the rug from under his feet. That would have been unpremeditated, of course, and done on a rather risky impulse. But Richard was angry with Mark that day, and in a very uncertain nervous condition.'

After a while Sally said: 'But the motive — the motive for premeditated murder of Mark? It doesn't really work out. Mark was opposing his marriage to Lisa, but he couldn't have prevented it. He could have cut him out of his will, but at the time the murder was planned there was no will in Richard's favour, and I can't see why he should have thought there was. And Mark wasn't even being difficult about Westwater.'

'I know. Mason must see that too. He may be assuming there was a sound motive somewhere, or he may feel that in Richard's case it isn't very necessary to prove one.'

'You mean that Richard — that he thinks Richard is insane?'

'I doubt if he'd go quite as far as that. But he may think him capable of getting things out of proportion. Lisa was trying to break off the engagement, you know, because of Mark's opposition. I don't know if Mason knows that, but Richard was evidently very frank with him about some things. Richard might possibly have felt that Mark's death was the only thing that could save his marriage.'

* * *

THEY REACHED FANCHESTER a little before three, and Mason received them at once. He was obviously unhappy, and he was very nice to them. But Lisa had told him about their investigations, and he argued, reluctantly, as Johnny had argued last night. Richard might have asked them to investigate with a view to clearing his own name, in the certainty that the case against George was unshakable. Johnny tried a little further argument, in the course of which it became fairly clear that the official mind had worked along much the same lines as his own, and at last Mason said: 'Listen, Mr Heldar. The Rover was seen near Westwater, as you know, between two-fifteen and two-thirty. At that time all the known suspects except Mr Willesdon were at Westwater. It's therefore a fair assumption — given the evidence of Mr Fenwick of Wolfram Mews — that Mr Willesdon was then driving it. It was seen again, going in the direction of London, at three-twenty-five. But Mr Willesdon was having tea in a Lyons' in West Kensington at four-forty-five or just after. He talked to one of the girls there. The Rover couldn't have got to West Kensington in an hour and twenty minutes from the west gate. Therefore Mr Willesdon was not driving it at three-twenty-five. It's again a fair assumption that Squadron Leader Thaxton was — the other suspects are all more or less accounted for at that time. And how did Mr Willesdon get back to London by four-forty-five, and how did the Armstrong get back, if he didn't drive it? To my mind we've proved collusion. Again, if Sir Mark was alive at three-five, Willesdon could barely have killed him and got to West Kensington by four-forty-five — even if he had the Armstrong waiting for him at the door.'

Johnny nodded slowly.

'I don't want you to build up false hopes for Miss Harz,' said Mason gravely. 'It's a bad business for her, but I'm afraid she's got to face it.'

Sally tried to face it herself all the way to Westwater,

but it wasn't easy. They found Lisa in the drawing room, and Christopher with her. He didn't look too pleased to see the Heldars, but Lisa came quickly to meet them. There were marks of tears on her face.

'Oh, Johnny!' she said. 'God be thanked you have come! Is there anything you can do? You have seen Mason?'

'Yes. I'm afraid there's nothing to be done there. I gather Christopher's been seeing him too.'

'Yes. He says the same thing. But surely there is something you can do?' She seemed to have more faith in Johnny than in Christopher.

'Look, Lisa,' said Johnny quietly. 'The police have got a practically water-tight case. Certain points are arguable, but Mason has a final answer for all the arguments. Richard and George together could have done it, and it's almost impossible that anyone else could. So, unless some new evidence turns up, I don't think there's anything we can do.'

'But you can try to find some new evidence. Please, Johnny!'

'Lisa,' said Johnny very gently, 'I doubt if there's any new evidence to find.'

Lisa turned her head away. 'You believe that Richard is guilty,' she said.

'Not necessarily. It's only that I honestly don't see how I can help.'

'Heldar's right, Lisa,' said Christopher. 'I know it's hard, my dear, but let it go at that, please. I'll brief the best man I can get. There's no certainty, you know, that Mason's case will convince a jury.'

Lisa let it go — but only, Sally was sure, for the moment. Christopher tried to persuade her to let him take her back to town, but she refused. Richard was in Fanchester, so she would stay here, and she hoped the Heldars would stay with her, at least for tonight.

When Christopher had gone, reluctantly, she looked at Johnny.

'You said a little while ago that it was almost impossible that anyone but Richard and George together should have murdered Mark. But you hesitated slightly in saying it. That, I think, was because Christopher was here?'

'To be honest, yes,' said Johnny.

'Because it is almost impossible that Deane or Colonel Danby did it. You would know if Deane were lying, and the evidence of Jakes must almost certainly clear the Colonel. He *could* not have reached the study before almost half-past three, and if Richard had left Mark alive, Mark must have fetched Christopher by that time. That is how you worked it out, yes? Very well. We are left with Richard and Christopher. And you wish to eliminate Christopher because he is a respectable English lawyer.'

'I admit it does rather boil down to that.'

'And because of that you will not accept the motives I suggested to Sally.'

'I find them a little hard to accept, Lisa. If I may say so, you haven't lived in England very long, and perhaps you don't know a great deal about English lawyers.'

'I know Christopher,' said Lisa slowly. 'What do you think lies behind that lawyer's mask of his? Do you know at all? I do not think so. But I know — not all, perhaps, but a good deal. He has a cool, quick brain, but he is capable of passion — and of anger. And if he had committed this murder, he would have been perfectly capable of returning to the drawing room, resuming his mask, taking up a magazine, and sitting quite still until the body was discovered. Perhaps he even hoped that Richard would be suspected. He opposed our explanation on the morning after the murder, which was to help Richard. He opposed your investigations, which were to disprove George's guilt. He has opposed every-thing we have tried to do. I beg you, Johnny, forget that he is an English lawyer, and think about Christopher.'

'I'll think about him as much as you like,' said Johnny. 'He could have done the murder — he could have done both murders. But I don't think anyone could prove that he did.'

'Nevertheless,' said Lisa obstinately, 'I ask you to think about him.'

CHAPTER NINE

Johnny lay awake till two o'clock obediently thinking about Christopher, and it didn't get him any further.

'I tried all sorts of lines,' he said, when they were lunching in the flat next day. 'I tried, among other things, to remember anything he'd said or done which seemed out of character — out of the character he's shown us, that is. I could think of only two things, and both of them *can* be explained by his concern for Lisa. The first was his donation of ten pounds, and the second was that he was so quick about offering to take George into Fanchester. He disliked George intensely, and yet he didn't give me a chance to sacrifice myself in his place. Well, that led me to think about the conversation which led up to his offer. I wondered if in the course of it, George could have said something which showed that he knew Christopher to be guilty. Said it deliberately — there was something just a little too ingenuous about him then, just as there was when he blackmailed us into bringing him back to tea. In that case Christopher might well have jumped at the opportunity of a *tête-à-tête*. I went over the conversation as well as I could remember it — I want you to check me in a minute — and although there was one possibly significant reference to Christopher, it seemed much more likely, on balance, that the whole thing was directed at Richard, as George's accomplice.

'By way of an opening, George asked if he could have the Rover. That puzzled Richard, but he replied, truthfully, that the Rover wasn't there. George then took the opportunity he had made of telling Richard that he had been seen entering the Rover's lock-up and had lied to the police about taking her out. Richard felt it would look a bit odd to carry George off for a private talk, and anyhow he'd had as much as he could take, so he tried to arrange to get him away, and probably leave him to get in touch again if he felt he must. The arrangement broke down, and Christopher, out of genuine concern for Lisa and Richard, stepped into the breach. Unfortunately he did it rather ungraciously, and provoked George's annoyance. That suggests a natural antipathy to George, but not at all necessarily that George had begun blackmailing operations. Then Lisa got short with George, and George got rude, partly because of the general attitude to him, but chiefly because he felt that his accomplice was letting him down. Then he made that very nasty crack about POW camps—'

'Concentration camps,' said Sally.

'Concentration camps? Are you sure? Yes, I believe you're right. But why concentration camps? Richard was presumably in a POW camp of some sort.'

'Perhaps George thought of it as a concentration camp. It must have been bad enough.'

'Perhaps. But George was a POW himself. I should have thought his mind would run on POW camps. Never mind. It's a small point. George then said goodbye, adding something or other about a restaurant called Emil's, where he wanted Lisa and Richard to dine with him, and which he suggested was a haunt of

Christopher's. I think that had some significance; it seemed rather dragged in, and there was rather a lot of it. But the significance may have been purely offensive. At the time I understood it to be a suggestion that both George and Christopher had been dining out with Richard's girl while Richard was languishing in his prison camp. Can you remember exactly what George did say?'

Sally recalled the appalling little scene: George standing at the door and smiling; Richard's white face. 'George said: "Let's dine at Emil's one night; I'm sure Dick would enjoy it. Even Sheringham approves of it, doesn't he?" Then I think he said the food was good, and then something about old Emil being full of reminiscences.'

'Full of reminiscences. That's odd, but I really don't see how there could be anything in it. I can't imagine how Emil could know anything about Mark's murder, whoever did it. The plan might possibly have been discussed in his restaurant, but whoever discussed it would take damn good care they weren't overheard. Unless, conceivably, George got tight.'

'George said something — just as he went out — about having a new after-dinner story. That might have meant something.'

'It might. But it probably meant something for Richard, rather than for anyone else.'

They finished the meal in silence and started on the washing-up. Sally said suddenly: 'You remember you had a theory that George didn't know who the murderer was, but only suspected, and came down to see if he could confirm his suspicions. It struck me vaguely after that that when he asked if he could have the Rover he might have been fishing for information. But that would imply that he was telling the truth when he said he found the Rover gone. Otherwise he wouldn't have needed any information about it. And he must have been lying — who else could have brought the Rover down?'

'Yes, I'm afraid that's no good. He must have—'

Johnny, who was extremely neat-handed, dropped the plate he was drying, ignored it when it broke on the edge of the sink, and stared at Sally.

* * *

A LITTLE AFTER seven o'clock that evening, Sally and Johnny walked up to a restaurant in Soho. It was a small place, and rather discreet; the windows were curtained, and above the door was painted the single word: 'Emil's'. It was the only restaurant of that name in the Telephone Directory.

Inside it was still discreet, and very quiet. The decorations were pleasant and unemphatic; the lights were subdued. It wasn't very expensive, but it was in quite good taste. At this comparatively early hour only a few tables were occupied.

A big, stout, middle-aged man came forward to meet them, his face wreathed in a professional smile.

'Good evening, Madame; good evening, Monsieur. Delighted to see you. And where would you like to sit?' He spoke with a heavy German accent.

'Somewhere rather quiet, I think,' said Johnny. 'In that corner, perhaps, if we may?'

'Certainly, Monsieur.' He shepherded them over to the table for two and drew out a chair for Sally. 'You will be cool here, near the electric fan.' Then he summoned a waiter, who also appeared to be German, and Johnny consulted Sally and ordered.

The food was very good indeed. So was the wine. Emil's was clearly a find from one point of view.

The restaurant filled up, and the big proprietor was

busy with other guests. But when the Heldars had reached the coffee stage he returned to them.

'Madame has enjoyed her dinner, I hope?'

'Very much indeed, thank you,' said Sally warmly.

'That is good. I think I have not had the pleasure of seeing Madame and Monsieur before, though I hope I shall see them again. Might I ask if someone has recommended my restaurant? I like to know my friends.'

'Yes,' said Johnny. 'A man we met a little while ago said that your restaurant was very good, and he was perfectly right. But I'm afraid he's now dead. You may have seen it in the papers. His name was George Willesdon.'

The professional smile faded, and the face took on the lines of a professional melancholy. This man was like Christopher, thought Sally, except that Christopher had only one mask, and Emil probably had a dozen. Was it only the masks themselves which suggested a certain wariness, as Christopher's did, or was there really a hint of caution in the dark eyes? Johnny had warned her that they would have to go very carefully; a restaurateur was always reluctant to involve himself, even remotely, in a police matter.

After the faintest pause Emil said: 'Yes, indeed. I have seen the news of poor Mr Willesdon's death. A most tragic affair. I am very sad.'

'I expect you knew him better than we did,' said Johnny. 'We only met him once. We were very much shocked by his death, and rather surprised.'

'I knew him — as one knows a client,' said Emil. 'He came here often enough, though I had not seen him for some weeks before this tragic event. I had the impression that he was not, perhaps, a very happy man. It is sometimes so with these young men who have been trained for war and find themselves at a loss in time of peace. Especially, I think, with those who have flown.

But I speak in ignorance, for I did not really know him.'

'We didn't know him either,' said Sally. 'But we — we're sorry for him.'

'I also, Madame.' He paused a moment. 'Madame and Monsieur met him shortly before his death?'

'The day before,' said Johnny.

'Indeed? It must then have come as a great shock. And as a surprise, I think Monsieur said? There were then no signs of his intention?'

'We thought not,' said Johnny, with the faintest emphasis on the first word.

'I see,' said Emil quietly. His eyes met Johnny's for a moment. Then he seemed to come to some decision. 'If Madame and Monsieur would wait a few minutes?' he murmured. 'I have one or two matters to attend to.' He drifted away to another table, wearing his smile again.

They waited for five minutes, and saw Emil speak to their waiter and go quietly out by the curtained doorway at the back. Presently the waiter came over and murmured in his turn. 'Monsieur Emil would be happy if Madame and Monsieur would join him for a liqueur in his office.'

'We shall be delighted,' said Johnny.

The waiter escorted them to the curtained doorway, into a narrow passage which, to judge by the noises off, led to the kitchen, and up an uncarpeted staircase. He opened a door at the top and showed them into a small, bare room.

Emil rose from behind a desk. 'I am very happy to see Madame and Monsieur. I hope they will give me the pleasure of drinking with me?'

He placed a chair for Sally, filled three liqueur glasses from a bottle of kirsch, and then drank gravely to her health. Then he looked at her and Johnny across the desk. He was still a little wary, but the obsequious air had gone, and so, thought Sally suddenly, had all the masks.

'I think,' he said quietly, 'you are Mr and Mrs Heldar.'

Johnny nodded. 'The papers?' he asked.

'Yes. The papers gave the names of those who were at Westwater Manor at the time of Sir Mark Mercator's death — among them, Mr and Mrs Heldar, who had previously carried out a successful private investigation in a case of murder. There was also a photograph of Madame, with certain others, on their way to attend the inquest upon Sir Mark. And you did not come here only because Willesdon said this was a good restaurant.'

'No,' said Johnny. He explained the situation very briefly, but very frankly. 'We believe that both Thaxton and Willesdon are innocent. But we have no proof, and something which Willesdon said on the day before his death suggested that you might possibly be able to help us. He implied — we think — that you knew something that no one else knew about one of the people concerned.'

Emil looked down into his glass. At last he said: 'It is true that I know something. But I do not know that it has anything to do with this matter, and in any case, I think it must also be known to the police.'

'I don't think the police know anything at all against the person we are thinking of,' said Johnny.

Emil frowned. 'They have found nothing among Sir Mark's papers?'

'I don't think so. There's been no indication of that.'

There was another silence. Then Emil said: 'Had I known this, I think I should have come forward. But I should have been reluctant to do so. You understand that I am in a difficult position. It is most undesirable for a restaurateur to be involved with the police. But you are not the police. Will you give me your word of honour that if, in your opinion, my knowledge cannot help Richard Thaxton, you will not repeat it to the police or to anyone else?'

'I give you my word,' said Johnny, 'that if I am entirely satisfied that it can't help Thaxton, it will never go beyond the three of us.'

Emil looked at him for a few moments. Then he nodded and began. 'Willesdon came here first in the summer of nineteen-forty-nine, soon after I had bought this restaurant. He came fairly often — when he had money. There were times when he had not. One evening in the early spring of nineteen-fifty he brought two friends, who were newly betrothed. It was a celebration. The young man was Richard Thaxton. The woman Willesdon introduced to me as Miss Harz, and he called her Lisa. But that is not the name she used when I first knew her. She was then Helga Forst. There is no mistake. She was plumper then, and her hair was different — her eyebrows too, I think. But I recognised her the moment she entered the restaurant.' His face had changed, and it no longer looked like India-rubber. The heavy jaw was set, and the mouth hard.

'If this had been my house — my home — she would never have entered it. But I am only a restaurateur, with my reputation to think of. So she sat there and ate and drank, and men looked at her. She seems' — he hesitated for a word — 'so *entzückend* — so charming. And so soft and gentle. And correct. *Immer korrekt.*' His voice was harsh and ugly.

'She did not know me, naturally. In the old days I was only one among a thousand — and I was unshaven, filthy, wasted away to nothing. But I knew her, and I could not entirely hide my emotion. She did not notice it, and Thaxton did not notice it — he was in love. But Willesdon noticed it. On the following evening he returned and asked me what I knew of her. I was still a little shaken — the sight of her had awakened memories which I had tried to bury for the sake of my sanity. Otherwise, perhaps, I would not have told him what I tell you now.

'I have Jewish blood, and for three years — the last three years of the war — I was in a concentration camp. Wolstein, *bei* Stuttgart. She came often to that camp. She was the mistress of the *Kommandant,* a man named Schleicher. He was bad — a man who loved cruelty for its own sake. But she was worse than he. She came to see—' He stopped, and said with a sudden quietness:

'Things that I will not speak of before Madame.'

After a little while Johnny said: 'Did Willesdon ever speak of her again?'

'I do not think so. And he never brought her here again. But she came here two or three times with another man. He was English — perhaps thirty-five years old — not very tall — fair — quite good-looking. A professional man: perhaps a lawyer. He was in love with her.'

'Yes,' said Johnny. 'We know him. Now, one last question. You told Sir Mark about her, and gave him something in writing?'

Again Emil was silent for a little. 'Is it necessary that I answer this, if Richard Thaxton is to be saved?'

'It is necessary. We must be able to prove that Sir Mark knew the truth.'

'Very well. I swore to him that I would say nothing, but I think it was for the sake of Richard Thaxton that he came to me. For the sake of Richard Thaxton, then, I will break my word. Sir Mark discovered, through certain of my Jewish friends, that I had been in Wolstein. He came to me in September, nineteen-fifty, and I gave him a signed statement about the woman — he showed me some photographs, and there was no doubt. He knew already that she had been at Wolstein, but he was gathering evidence from several people. I think I was the only one in England. There must, then, have been other statements besides mine. Sir Mark spoke of a man in Germany — an old friend of his — whom I had known in the camp: a Jew named Klaus Mandelbaum. But you tell me that no statements have been found. No doubt she has seen to that.' He paused again and swept one of his big hands over his forehead, in a gesture of great weariness. 'If it is necessary — and your faces tell me that it is — I will tell this story to the police.'

* * *

SALLY HAD RUNG up Lisa in the afternoon — very reluctantly, and with an obscure distaste for her own deception — and told her they had a business engagement for the evening and wouldn't be able to get back tonight. They hadn't rung up Wainwright, for the gossip of the Danesfield exchange might have got round to Westwater, and they took care not to arrive at the Arms before closing time. But Wainwright seemed thankful to see them. His friendly face was sharpened by anxiety, and he looked very tired. They gathered that for two evenings his public bar had been the focus of bitter indignation meetings on behalf of Richard Thaxton. Even the Colonel, who was going about like a roaring lion and apparently doing his best to intimidate the Chief Constable, had relieved his feelings in the bar parlour, and Wainwright was beginning to feel the strain. Johnny reassured him as far as possible, and he gave them a room for the night. The bed was quite comfortable, but neither of them slept much.

After breakfast, at Johnny's request, Wainwright took them along to the Post Office and introduced them to the girl on the telephone exchange — who, as it happened, had been on duty on the evening before George's death. She was quite ready to talk.

'Yes, Mr Heldar. There were two calls for the manor between six and seven — they're down here in the record. They were both from call boxes in Fanchester. The first one was at twenty-five past six, and it was for Miss Harz. It was a foreign gentleman phoning.'

'A foreign gentleman?' asked Johnny.

'Yes. I think he was German. He spoke to Mr Fenton in English, when Mr Fenton answered the phone, but he had a very foreign accent, and he said his name was Mr...Mr...Smit, it sounded like. Not Smith.'

'Would it be Schmidt?'

'Yes, I think that was it. He asked for Miss Harz, and Mr Fenton sounded a bit doubtful — I think perhaps he thought the gentleman was a reporter putting on an act.' The girl hesitated and flushed a little. 'I shouldn't have been listening, of course.'

'I'm glad you did. Please go on.'

'Well, Mr Fenton said he'd inform Miss Harz, and after a few minutes she came on the line. The gentleman spoke to her in a foreign language — it sounded like German, and Miss Harz is German, isn't she? Besides, before he rang off, he said: "Heil Hitler!" They talked for quite a while — he had nine minutes altogether, what with Mr Fenton talking to him first and having to fetch Miss Harz. But I didn't understand any of the other words. Only the gentleman didn't sound very nice; he was talking quite quietly, but there was a nasty sort of tone in his voice. And Miss Harz was kind of sharp with him at first, and then she got sort of quiet and confidential.'

'Tell me this. Are you quite sure the gentleman really was German? When he talked German, was there anything to suggest that it might be a foreign language to him?'

The girl considered. 'Well, yes, I suppose it might have been. He spoke slower than Miss Harz. At first, that was. And then she began to speak slower, and once or twice he asked her something, and I think she repeated what she'd been saying.'

'I see,' said Johnny. 'And the second call, Miss Hadley?'

The second call had made Miss Hadley very angry. She told them all about the reporter who had told Fenton he was one of Richard's old squadron, and then offered Richard five hundred pounds for the inside stories of Mercator's murder and the prison camp in China.

CHAPTER TEN

Three-quarters of an hour later the Heldars were in Mason's office, and Johnny was talking. Mason listened, at first politely, and then with an anxious concentration.

'If she had left her flat immediately after Willesdon telephoned to her, she could have been in Wolfram Mews before him. I understand Fenwick saw him at about twelve-fifteen. We tried it out, on foot, yesterday afternoon, and we did it in a quarter of an hour, walking fast. We could have had the Rover out and away in another three minutes at the outside.

'She could have reached the waterman's cottage between two-fifteen and two-thirty. She probably knew the place, because she and Thaxton wandered about a lot when they were at Westwater after Mercator's accident, and I remember Thaxton's saying they'd been over every inch of the estate. We found no trace of footprints on the track which leads to the cottage, but she probably walked on the grass in the middle. She couldn't avoid leaving traces of the Rover, but that wouldn't matter very much, because even if they were identified the Rover could be interpreted in various ways. But she couldn't risk leaving prints which would obviously be a woman's.

'After that she crossed the park and waited at some point within sight of the north avenue — and possibly the courtyard — to see when Thaxton left. Or possibly not the courtyard: she'd have seen Sheringham's car there, and probably recognised it, and it might have made her change her plans. Anyhow, as soon as Thaxton had gone, she made a circuit by way of the park — she couldn't risk appearing on the lawns — and reached the study somewhere between three o'clock and five past. She hoped to find Mercator alone, but if she didn't, she could explain her presence by saying she had come to make a last appeal to him. He was alone, however — probably because he had been shaken by his quarrel with Thaxton and hadn't recovered sufficiently to fetch Sheringham. She gave him one more chance to agree to her marriage with Thaxton, and Deane overheard his answer.

'She then killed him, using the blow we discussed at the beginning of all this. It could have been used successfully by a woman, if she'd been properly taught, and she may have learnt it in the concentration camp at Wolstein. She saw the will on his table — or perhaps he had shown it to her — and took it from a motive which she later ascribed, rather improbably, to Sheringham.' Johnny explained the motive. 'If there were no hope of setting aside the restraining clause, then it would be safer to destroy a will which might possibly indicate a motive for murder on her part. If Sheringham's opinion — which she could get on a hypothetical case — were favourable, then she could allow the will to be found. In any case, her hand was rather forced by the fact that Thaxton turned out to have seen the will and told you about it; if it hadn't turned up, his position would have been even worse than it was.

'She returned to the waterman's cottage and drove off in the Rover, which was seen by Danby at the west gate at three-twenty-five. There is, of course, a difficulty here. I doubt if she could have hoped to establish any convincing alibi; she probably relied much more on her apparent lack of motive and on the general improbability of her being involved. But Thaxton should have reached London well before her — he had the Armstrong and about forty minutes' start on the more direct road — and he might well go straight to her flat. She wouldn't want him to find her out. It was just a chance that he was held up by nerves, and even so it must have been a very near thing. She'd have to put the Rover away when she got to town. Incidentally, she'd have to take a chance on being seen in the mews at a time when people are coming home from work, but she seems to have got away with that.'

'Yes,' said Mason slowly. 'Well, it's true she hasn't got an alibi. I went into that, as a matter of routine. She said she was at home all afternoon, from the time Willesdon phoned her until just after five-thirty, when she went to a couple of shops near her flat and bought some food. The people at the shops confirm that. And, as a matter of fact, Thaxton said he had intended to call on an RAF friend in Richmond on his way back but decided not to because he was so shaken.'

'She may have suggested that call. At least, she almost certainly knew he meant to pay it. She did her shopping on the way back from the mews, and if he was on the doorstep when she got home, she'd just been out to get something for supper. If he'd cut out the call and got there earlier, he wouldn't have been likely to hang about indefinitely, and she'd just happened to be out for a walk, or perhaps washing her hair or something, when he rang. It's good enough.'

'It hangs together,' said Mason. 'But you haven't given me any proof yet, Mr Heldar.'

'I know,' said Johnny. 'I can only go on. The motive for the first murder is clear now. Miss Harz has shown a tendency to attribute her own motives, suitably edited, to other people — or, more specifically, to Sheringham.' He repeated the story of Mark's alleged accusation of Lisa and Christopher. 'It interested me, because it suggested a far more likely reason for Mercator's opposition to the marriage than the mere fact that Miss Harz was German, and I felt that some very good reason must exist. I believe that she was alone with Mercator for a minute or two, as she said, on the afternoon of his accident, and that he told her — or perhaps reminded her — that he knew of her connection with the concentration camp, and said that unless she broke off the engagement herself he would show Thaxton documentary proof of that connection.'

'Wait a minute,' said Mason. 'Are you suggesting that she managed to get hold of the signed statements Emil talked about?'

'That's possible, but I don't think so. If those statements had still been in existence, I don't believe she'd have killed Mercator unless she had known beyond doubt where they were — and that she'd be able to get at them — and he was much too shrewd to have told her where they were. If he showed them to Thaxton, Thaxton would certainly refuse to marry her, and Mercator, being a man of influence, might conceivably make England too hot to hold her — though I doubt that. But the law couldn't touch her — there's no reason to think she's a War Criminal — and at the worst she could make a future for herself elsewhere. If, on the other hand, she murdered Mercator and the statements came to light, she would probably hang.' Johnny paused.

'This is very largely conjecture,' he said slowly. 'Mercator was a very fair man and attached great importance to being fair. Thaxton implied that he had some trouble with his conscience over a certain amount of anti-German feeling. He collected these statements before Thaxton was shot down, and with the object of persuading him not to marry Miss Harz — he probably knew that nothing short of documentary evidence would convince him. After Thaxton was shot down, he may have felt that, if he took any action against Miss Harz, it would be only to serve his own prejudice. So I suggest that he destroyed the documents. Whether he was right or wrong isn't for us to say; it was his decision. I think, too, that when he heard Thaxton was alive he took no immediate steps to replace the documents. Perhaps he hoped Thaxton wouldn't return to Miss Harz. After all, he'd been away for more than four years, and must now be far older in experience. But the moment Mercator saw the two of them together he knew that Thaxton was as much in love as ever. When they arrived on the day of his accident, my wife and I both noticed that he was curiously shaken.

'I suggest that when he was alone with Miss Harz, he told her that he had destroyed the documents, but that he proposed to obtain copies. In the first instance it must have taken him some time to collect the documents; it would mean long and perhaps difficult enquiries in German. I dare say he had agents there, and Jewish contacts. But getting hold of copies would be much simpler and quicker, in some cases at any rate, because he'd know where to go. Now, Emil mentioned a man called Klaus Mandelbaum, who had probably provided one of the statements. You asked us, Inspector, if we had heard Mercator speak of a man called Klaus.'

'I did,' said Mason. 'There was an unfinished letter under the blotter on Sir Mark's table, in his own writing. We imagined he'd hidden it because he'd been interrupted — probably by his murderer. It was in German, but I got it translated, and it said something like this: 'Dear Klaus, I am sorry to trouble you again, but I am beginning to wonder if you have received my letter of August 4th.' That was all, and no surname or address.'

'I see,' said Johnny. 'Yes, that fits in. Well, this again is largely conjecture, but it's what I believe to have happened on the day of Mercator's accident — the fourth. As soon as Thaxton had left him, having refused to reconsider the engagement, he wrote a short letter to Klaus, asking for a new statement. It would have been quicker to go to London and see Emil, but perhaps he meant to do that too; he may have felt that it would take the word of more than one man to convince Thaxton. In any case, he came out of the study and put his letter on the table at the foot of the stairs, where the outgoing post is normally left. He probably thought Thaxton and Miss Harz had gone, and why they hadn't I don't know. Thaxton must have been in the car, or at any rate outside, and she may have come back for something. She saw Mercator standing on the rug, and he didn't see her; perhaps she was out of his range of vision, or perhaps she was in a shadowy part of the hall; the light under the staircase is dim at that time of day, and his sight was poor. She saw him put the letter on the table and guessed that it concerned her. I'm not suggesting, of course, that this was a premeditated attempt; she just saw an opportunity, thought very quickly, and took it. Supposing she pulled the rug sharply from under his feet. She obviously couldn't count on solving her problem for good and all, though a man of his age might possibly break a thigh in such a fall and die of shock or pneumonia. But there was a very fair chance that he would be laid out, and that she would be able to get hold of the letter. He would probably never realise that it hadn't been posted, and she would at least gain a few days. And if he was laid out, he probably wouldn't remember the few minutes before his fall, and so wouldn't remember — even if he had realised it at the time — that the rug had been pulled from under him.

'She took a risk, of course. But as it turned out, the risk was amply justified. I suggest that Mercator did remember what had happened, and guessed that she had been responsible, and that that was one reason why he was in such a hurry to make a new will. He knew there would probably be a second attempt, and he didn't want to cut Thaxton out if he could possibly help it. I talked to my own solicitor yesterday afternoon — I put a hypothetical case — and he says that, to judge by his own experience, even a businessman might well fail to realise that a clause "in restraint of marriage" could almost certainly be set aside. A man — and particularly a man who is powerful in his own way — finds it very hard to realise that he can't tie up his money exactly as he wants to, especially if he wants it very badly. I don't suppose Mercator thought for one moment that the new will would prevent Thaxton from marrying Miss Harz, but if the restraining clause had been incontestable it might have prevented Miss Harz from marrying Thaxton. As he saw it, it was the only thing he could do, either as a temporary measure to prevent the marriage until he had his proof from Klaus, or as a permanent measure if he died and for some reason the proof failed to come to light. So, in a way, he played into Miss Harz's hands.'

Johnny paused again and lit a cigarette. He was

frowning heavily, and Sally knew he was hating what he had to do.

'Well, after she had killed Mercator, Willesdon intervened. We know that he'd heard about her past from Emil, and I suggest that he'd been blackmailing her ever since. It probably wasn't blackmail for money — at least, not on any large scale. He couldn't have got her into very serious trouble by revealing her past — and if he could I don't suppose he'd have lived to do it. Goods and services, as and when required, were more in his line. The use of the Rover, long after she might have sold it; a free lock-up even after she'd left the mews; a letter to Thaxton, suggesting Willesdon for the land-agency; Willesdon kept on, after he'd been proved incompetent, until she sold Westwater. But once he knew she was guilty of murder it was a different matter.'

Johnny outlined the conversation on the afternoon before George's death, and then went on.

'He probably assumed, as he said, that Thaxton had taken the Rover, and when the police questioned him about it, he suspected that Thaxton was the murderer, and came to Westwater to confirm his suspicions. But he realised that Thaxton was telling the truth when he said he'd come down in the Armstrong; that statement would be confirmable by witnesses. So he knew that Miss Harz was guilty, and he told her so. He did it quite cleverly because everything he said seemed to be directed at Thaxton. "Poor old Dick's not in a very nice position." That was probably the first hint. "People who come out of concentration camps." We all thought he meant POW camps, but he meant precisely what he said — a reminder to Miss Harz that he knew about her past. The rather laboured references to Emil and his restaurant were a further reminder. And finally, just as he went out: "I've got a new after-dinner story." That, on top of the rest, told her the truth. She was extremely shaken, but she was wise enough to make no attempt to hide it and allow us all to think that it was on Thaxton's behalf.

'After that she developed a headache and didn't reappear till dinner time. I remember thinking it was unlike her to desert Thaxton at a time like that. But she must have wanted to be alone to think things out. She must have been alone when Fenton came to tell her she was wanted on the telephone.' Johnny repeated the switchboard girl's evidence. 'Thaxton may have known about the call; Fenton may have looked for her in the drawing room. But she could have found some story for Thaxton. I'm satisfied that the caller was Willesdon; since he was a POW he may well have spoken German after a fashion, and the "Heil Hitler!" was a characteristic touch. Perhaps she promised him money; at any rate she persuaded him to meet her at the dam.

'The next morning, when Danby came and told us he'd found the body, she tried, not very reasonably, to prevent me from going back with him. She wanted me to stay and talk to Thaxton, to prevent his hearing about it. I think she remembered that I had recognised the blow which killed Mercator and was afraid I might be able to tell that Willesdon had been murdered. In which she overestimated me, I'm afraid. I guessed that Willesdon might have been knocked out, but I could find no evidence for it. In fact I was almost certainly wrong, because I don't believe a woman, however expert, could actually knock out a man of Willesdon's age. But she could have used one of two or three Judo blows which would send him over into the water, and which are designed partially to disable a man for a short time.' Johnny went into brutal details, getting them over as soon as possible. 'In the case of a man who was in poor condition because of prolonged drinking, they would have a greater effect. He would probably become practically unconscious, and so unable to struggle. The cold water might have revived him; on the other hand, it might have increased the shock. In any case, he almost certainly wouldn't be able to call for help.'

There was a long silence. At last Mason said: 'Anything else, Mr Heldar?'

'Her behaviour all along. We all thought she was fighting for Thaxton, and up to a point she was, but she was fighting primarily for herself. At first, I think, she was prepared to let Thaxton take the consequences; she probably got him down to Westwater on the day of the first murder partly for that purpose, and partly because she had in any case to get rid of him for the afternoon. They both said she had tried to break off her engagement over the weekend, because of Mercator's opposition, and Thaxton indicated that he came down because he knew he must talk his uncle round if he weren't going to lose her. So she'd paved the way quite nicely for a quarrel. When she planned the first murder, you see, she didn't know there would be any chance of Thaxton's inheriting Mercator's estate. She couldn't wait for Mercator to make a new will, and she probably thought he wouldn't, anyway, as long as Thaxton was engaged to her. And Thaxton was quite well off, but not wealthy. Then the new will appeared. But Thaxton couldn't inherit if he were convicted of murder; the law wouldn't allow him — or his heirs — to benefit by his crime. So she had to protect him, which made things much easier for her, for it gave her a cover behind which she could fight for herself. She had him pronounced unfit for interrogation, and then she organised a general pooling of information by the known suspects, so that she could find out exactly where she and he stood. Then she had a heart-to-heart talk with my wife and offered her false information and improbable suggestions about Sheringham. I think, being a foreigner, she genuinely didn't realise how improbable they were. I dare say she would have been quite satisfied if Deane or Danby had been found guilty. But she was very careful what she said about Willesdon, until she had silenced him. If Willesdon had got into serious trouble with the police, he wouldn't have hesitated to tell you about her past. After that she thought she was sitting pretty; she wasn't seriously worried by our investigations, and she was clever enough not to raise too many objections to them. But finally, when Thaxton was arrested, she over-reached herself. She should have let it go at that, but she put us on to Sheringham — the only other suspect who might still have been guilty. And if we hadn't been thinking about Sheringham, we should probably never have thought about her.'

* * *

MASON RANG up Johnny in the evening and made a brief report. The next day was Saturday, and they went to see him again, by invitation, in the afternoon, and heard his full story.

'Squadron Leader Thaxton's statement supports your theory of how the accident happened. He went along to the drawing room to fetch her, and she asked him about his interview with Sir Mark. They were there nearly five minutes — she probably wanted to be sure he hadn't been told anything. Then she said she must go upstairs for a minute, and he said he'd wait in the car — he didn't want to meet Sir Mark again. He waited nearly another five minutes, and then she came out. It's nothing like evidence, but personally I'm fairly satisfied. Fenton can't remember what letters were left out that afternoon, but we're getting in touch with Klaus Mandelbaum, and I expect we shall find that he never received a letter from Sir Mark written on that day. He may be able to give us some more information about Miss Harz's past, too.'

'Her Wolstein past,' said Johnny. 'But I've been wondering how she got to this country. She'd been here for some years, and it wasn't easy for Germans to get in soon after the war.'

'I've made some enquiries about that. She changed her name, as you know. In her position she was probably able to take on a new identity at the end of the war — possibly a genuine identity belonging to some girl who had died in the concentration camp. Anyway, after she became Lisa Harz, she married a Canadian officer. It was quite soon after the war, and the Services were still not supposed to marry German girls, but they got away with it somehow. He brought her to England, and then went back to Canada himself and divorced her. The marriage may have been simply a temporary arrangement to get her out of Germany and give her a safe nationality. Squadron Leader Thaxton knew about it; she'd told him some pathetic story about being deserted. He'd told Sir Mark about it, but no one else, which was natural enough, and as she'd gone back to her supposed maiden name no one suspected it. After the divorce she started as a photographer's model — oh, entirely respectable; for advertisements and that sort of thing — and then she became a dress model and went right to the top. She took a slight risk, because someone who had known her as Helga Forst might have recognised one of her photographs. But that wasn't very likely, in this country, and Emil said she had altered her appearance a bit.'

Mason paused for a moment. He looked tired and very human.

'I oughtn't to say it, of course, but I'm thanking Heaven it ended the way it did. Of course she deserved to hang— — he murders were as callous and cold-

blooded as any I ever heard of. There were no extenu-
ating circumstances at all. But I'm thankful for
Squadron Leader Thaxton's sake. I doubt if he'd have
stood up to the trial.'

'Are we allowed to ask how she managed it?' said
Johnny.

'She had a small capsule of cyanide concealed under
a sort of glass jewel on the top of her lipstick case. Very
ingenious. I had thought of some sort of suicide pill, in
view of her history — some of the Nazis had them, you
remember — and I was keeping an eye on her. But I
hadn't been able to search her because I hadn't got to
the point of charging her. I'm afraid she just waited
until she was sure I knew too much, and she wasn't
going to get away with it. She'd been putting on an act
all along, being very courageous in the face of a false
accusation, and she just said quietly: "Very well; I will
go with you. That is what you want, isn't it?" Then she
took out her compact and her lipstick and started
making up her face. It didn't even look like bravado; it
looked as if she was just preparing for the journey.
She'd swallowed the stuff before I could do anything.'

Presently Sally said: 'I suppose Squadron Leader
Thaxton's at Westwater, Inspector?'

Mason nodded. 'As far as I know. He's all alone
there, too, apart from the servants — even Mr Deane's
gone away. It's funny; he took it much more quietly
than I'd have expected. I thought I'd have a job convincing him that she'd done it, but he seemed to accept
it fairly easily. Mr Sheringham took it much harder —
on the surface.'

As they drove out of the town Sally said: 'I couldn't
be more thankful it ended the way it did, but wasn't it a
little unwise of Mason to let her know she hadn't a
chance before he was in a position to search her?'

'Well, she was very clever,' said Johnny. 'Possibly a

quicker brain than Mason's. Or possibly not. For instance, it isn't really certain that she wouldn't have got
away with it. If you think about it, there's really no
proof at all.'

Sally had to think about it for a minute or two before its possible implications began to dawn on her.

* * *

THEY HAD no desire to go to Westwater, but their luggage had to be collected. They had no intention of
bothering Richard; they were responsible for what had
happened to him, and if he ever wanted to see them
again, it wouldn't be this weekend.

It was half-past five when they drove up to the
house, and the courtyard was in shadow. The front
door stood open. Johnny rang, and after a minute or
two Fenton came. He actually smiled a little when he
saw them.

'Good evening, madam. Good evening, sir. Very
glad to see you again. Mr Richard is in the library, I
believe.'

'We won't disturb Mr Richard, Fenton,' said Sally.
'We've just come for our luggage.'

'Mr Richard anticipated that you would do so,
madam. He hoped to see you as soon as you arrived.'

Richard's sense of duty, thought Sally miserably.
They would have to go through with it now — all of
them.

Richard was so haggard that he looked almost old.
But he rose quickly and smiled at them.

'Come along in,' he said. 'I'm glad to see you. Will
you bring some drinks, please, Fenton?'

Sally didn't quite know what she answered. Richard
drew up a chair for her, and when Fenton had gone
looked at her for a moment.

'It's all right, you know,' he said gently. 'I was afraid you might try to run away, but I hope you won't.' Then he passed round cigarettes.

When the drinks arrived, he dispensed them. Then he sat down and smiled at Sally again.

'It's not quite as bad as you think,' he said.

'Isn't it, Richard?'

'No.' He was very grave now. 'I'd like to explain, partly because it would help me, and partly because I hope it would help you a little. I don't want you to feel that the damage is beyond repair. It is bad, of course — which is not your fault. If anyone is to blame for the whole thing, it's me, because I got involved with Lisa in the first place. No, it's all right — I'm not getting a guilt complex. But the damage might be worse, because I wasn't really as much in love with Lisa as you all thought I was.' He broke off for a moment, and looked out of the window, frowning a little.

'Before I went to Korea, I was quite desperately in love with her. I was ten or fifteen years younger in experience then. And while I was away, I went on being desperately in love with her. The idea of Lisa kept me going in the POW camp. It was a totally false idea, of course, but that didn't matter. The point was that it did keep me going, and nothing else could have done. I shall always be rather grateful to her for that. But when I came back, it was different. For the first day or two it was all right — there was a glamour over everything, and when my nerves kept quiet, I felt rather like a god on a shiny cotton-wool cloud. All slightly unreal. Then the haze began to lift, and I began to realise that Lisa wasn't quite the person I had thought she was. I don't mean that I felt there was anything wrong about her; she just wasn't my idea of Lisa. I refused to admit it at first; I told myself it was just the state of my nerves. Then when it gained ground a bit, I argued that after all it was I who had changed, not she; I had outgrown her. That wasn't her fault. She had been faithful to me for four and a half years, during most of which she had believed I was dead — in my saner moments I knew she had never been in love with Christopher. And she was still in love with me — I thought. That was a rather remarkable record for any woman, and an amazing record for such an attractive one. She was extraordinarily patient with my nerves, and after Mark was killed, she seemed to be frightened to death for me, and moving mountains to get me cleared. So what could I do? I was still in love with her, up to a point, and even if I hadn't been, it would have been quite impossible to back out. I told myself that in most marriages the glamour wears off, and that I was really damned lucky.' He broke off again. 'So you see — it isn't as bad as all that. And at least' — he shivered a little and his voice grew brittle — 'we're spared the trial.'

Johnny, moving quickly but without apparent hurry, took it upon himself to get another round of drinks. They talked quietly about nothing in particular until Richard's voice was normal again, and then Sally said: 'Are you going to stay here, Richard, or come back to town, or what?'

'Stay here, I think,' he said. 'I don't know exactly what the legal position is, but as far as I can see the place is mine now either way. Mark's last will... There's plenty of work here. I can carry on with his improvements, and I shan't get another agent.' He hesitated. 'If you don't dislike the idea too much, I hope you'll come down sometimes. But if you don't feel like it, I shall quite understand.'

'We'd love to come,' said Sally. She hesitated too, and then went on: 'If you'd like us to stay this weekend, we'd like to. But if you'd rather not, you know us well enough to say so.' The inquest on Lisa was to be held on

Monday. Richard wouldn't be needed, but his sense of duty might drag him to it. Johnny might be able to stop him, or at the worst they might be able to go with him.

'I should like it very much,' he said at once. 'But are you sure…?'

'Quite sure,' said Sally.

After a little Richard said: 'I know Mark would like to think you were here. By the way, has Christopher been in touch with you about the will?'

'How do you mean?'

'Evidently he hasn't. No doubt he will be. You never wondered why Mark didn't ask you to witness it, instead of his nurses?'

'No,' said Sally, still a little puzzled.

'Well, it's not really for me to tell you, but Christopher must be used to my indiscretions by now. You couldn't witness it because you benefit under it. He wanted you to have your pick of the furniture and ornaments he brought from Hampstead, and he urged his executors to encourage you to pick as much as you wanted.'

Sally was quite unable to answer, but Richard seemed to understand.

'So I've got an excellent excuse for bringing you down again,' he said gently.

THE MAN WHO
WASN'T THERE

CHAPTER ONE

"What are you going to do this afternoon?" asked Sally Heldar.

"Well, I finished the potatoes this morning," said Johnny. "I want to do the lettuces and peas." He looked up at the oak beams which ran across the kitchen ceiling and added with studied detachment: "I had hoped my wife might help me."

"It might be done," said Sally gravely. "After a decent interval."

They washed up the lunch dishes and then went into the sitting room. It wasn't warm enough to sit outside, but it was a perfect April day. The daffodils were out in the little garden, and the apple blossom made a pink froth over the old brick walls and thrust up against the clear blue sky. Inside there were daffodils too, bright against the dark panelling and the old oak furniture. Sally was suddenly profoundly grateful, not for the first time, to Johnny's Great-Aunt Charlotte, who had left them this cottage. Johnny was sitting opposite her, wearing the appalling flannel trousers in which he gardened, a disreputable tweed jacket, a khaki shirt which was falling to pieces, and no tie. He looked entirely contented. Beyond the little window which opened on to the lawn, she could see Peter, peacefully asleep in his pram. All was utterly right with the world.

The telephone on the little table beside her rang sharply. She lifted the receiver, slightly annoyed and very faintly anxious. As a rule, no one rang them up at weekends.

"Minningham 2048," she said.

"Sally, I'm frightfully sorry to bother you but I wondered if I might come down this afternoon."

It took her a moment or two to recognise Tim's voice — even to place it as a Heldar voice. Tim Heldar was Johnny's cousin but, for all practical purposes, more like a younger brother. She wondered if there was something wrong with the line. Then she realised that it wasn't that.

"I want to talk to you both rather urgently, if you don't mind," he was saying.

"Of course, Tim. Come along. Would you like to stay the night?"

"No, thanks very much. Just an hour or so. I've got to get back to town before dinner. I'll be with you about half past three."

"Good," said Sally. "We'll be here."

She put down the receiver. Johnny said: "What's the matter, darling?"

"I don't know, but something is. I think we're probably going to hear about this girl at last."

"That'll be a relief," said Johnny.

They knew there was a girl, and they knew that for the first time in Tim's life it was serious, and that was all. Tim was probably unaware that they knew even that. But for the last two months they had seen him undergoing the solemn ecstasies of a young man deeply in love. They had also seen that he was desperately worried. It wasn't, they were certain, simply the fear that his love might go unreturned. It wasn't — or it wasn't only — the prospect of responsibility. There was more to it than that. It wasn't their business unless, and until, he chose to tell them about it, but they had begun to wonder if he could cope with it himself. He was twenty-four years old, but he hadn't grown up, as they had, under the forcing influences of war. Two years in the peace-time Army and three at Oxford, and the last year in a quiet, if world-famous, family firm of antiquarian booksellers hadn't made him any older than his age.

* * *

THEY HAD PLANTED the lettuces and peas and were getting clean again when they heard the familiar noises of Tim's old Morris in the lane. When he came into the narrow hall, Sally was shocked. Tim looked older than his age today. His thick corn-coloured hair, his china-blue eyes, fine features, and clear skin made most people take him for a young undergraduate. Now he was pale and heavy-eyed, as if he hadn't slept, and he looked almost like a man of thirty.

He was making a painful effort to be calm and matter-of-fact. He accepted a cigarette, lit it, and after several unsuccessful attempts at a start, said abruptly and more loudly than he had intended: "I came to tell you I'm hoping to be married soon."

"Good," said Sally gently. "But it's not quite working out; is that it, Tim?"

"Oh, it'll work out all right in the end," he said unhappily. "At least, I think so. But at the moment everything's in the most bloody mess. She's in trouble, and she won't tell me about it properly, so I can't help her. And even if I knew all about it, I'm not sure I could get her out of it. Only I think Johnny might."

"Let's have it then," said Johnny quietly.

Tim looked gratefully at him, and then began.

"Her name's Prudence Thorpe, and I met her at a party two months ago. Her people live in Northamptonshire, and they're more or less county. 'More or less' is what she says. Her father's people were manufacturers somewhere in Yorkshire, and unfortunately they're frightfully rich."

"I wouldn't worry about that," said Sally. No one could look at Tim now and think for a moment that he was interested in Prudence Thorpe's money.

Tim managed to return Sally's smile. "I do a bit," he said. "But that's unimportant compared with the rest of it. Well, Prue went to a very expensive school and then Paris, and when she came home her mother wanted her to stay there and take her place in the marriage market. But she didn't want that, and she insisted on doing a secretarial course in London — Mrs Wisbech's. When she finished, about three months ago, she got a job almost at once and largely on the strength of having good French. It was with a man called Frodsham who lives — lived — in Richmond."

Johnny made no movement, but Sally was aware of a sudden alertness in him. Tim went on. "He was English by birth — that's to say, his father was English — but his mother is French. I believe his father was an artist and spent most of his time in Paris. At any rate, Frodsham himself was born and brought up there, and never came to England until about four years ago when he must have been fortyish. So he was" — Tim's jaw hardened a little — "entirely French in all essentials. Well, he and his mother came over here — I don't know why — and he bought a house in Richmond. Or it may be technically Twickenham. It's on the Middlesex bank. He appears to have had money; at any rate, he didn't do anything for a living. But for his own amusement he was writing a book. A book on diabolism in France. He was writing it in French, and he wanted an intelligent secretary with good French to type it and do some of his research for him. His credentials must have been adequate because Prue got the job through Mrs Wisbech's. That was good enough for her people, and it was very naturally good enough for Prue herself. She's led a pretty sheltered existence, and she's very inexperienced."

Sally didn't look at Johnny. But Heaven send, she thought, Tim would never have cause to revise that naively expressed opinion.

"At first," he said, "she quite liked Frodsham. I gather he had a certain amount of charm. And she thought his interest in diabolism — including its nastier aspects — was entirely scientific and detached. But she's no fool, and after a little she began to realise it wasn't. Oh, I don't mean he celebrated the Black Mass or anything like that. But his interest was not detached. He also had an interest in various women — Prue heard him on the telephone once or twice — and particularly in one woman who lived in Richmond and had a husband. What's more" — Tim's jaw hardened again — "Frodsham tried to take an interest in Prue herself. She thought she could cope with him, of course. And though she didn't like the situation, she didn't want to leave. It was a matter of self-respect; she didn't want to admit failure. And she was afraid that if she had to tell her people the job hadn't been a success they'd want her to come home. She's not of age — she's not twenty yet — and her father's a bit old-fashioned, and her mother seems to be a very silly woman.

"Well, that was how things stood when I met her, and a little after that she told me all about it. I told her she must leave Frodsham at once. I said I wanted to marry her, and if she would, there would be no question of failure. She had only to say she was leaving to be married. But I'm afraid I made rather a mess of it. I was very angry with Frodsham, and I didn't stop to think it out. So I was a bit high-handed, I think."

"I've no doubt you were," said Sally. "It's a very marked Heldar failing. It sometimes works though."

Tim grinned. "It didn't this time," he said. "Besides, my suggestion wasn't altogether tactful in itself. I was offering her a way out, and she didn't want any way out."

Sally looked thoughtfully at him. This sort of perception was new in him. Was it possible that, after all, this experience had matured him?

"We had a bit of a row," he went on. "But I was more cautious after that, and Frodsham got rather more difficult, and last Tuesday evening she said she'd marry me. It was a bit awkward — her people were so well off, and I'd got nothing but my salary — but it seemed the only thing to do."

It would, thought Sally. In Tim, the Heldar passion for chivalry was still almost entirely untempered by the second thoughts of experience.

"She said she'd give Frodsham notice the next day," he continued. "A fortnight's notice — she insisted it couldn't be less. And then the next evening she told me she'd changed her mind. At least, she seemed to think she'd be leaving Frodsham, but she went back on our engagement. Not finally, I gathered, but at any rate for the time being. She gave me a lot of reasons — we were both rather young; she wanted to be independent for a while before she married and so on. But none of them was the real reason. I'm quite sure something had actually happened that day to make her change her mind. She was very worried and upset, and she looked as if she'd had a shock of some sort. But she wouldn't tell me what it was. After a lot of persuasion, she agreed to see me again the following evening. And then the next day she rang me up at the shop about half past five and said she had a cold and couldn't come out. She didn't sound as if she had a cold, but there was nothing I could do about it, and she wouldn't fix another evening.

"Well, that was Thursday. On Friday evening — yesterday — I bought an evening paper on my way home, and I saw that Frodsham had been murdered the night before."

Johnny nodded. "I saw it too," he said. "It didn't mean anything, of course."

"No. Well, I went straight to Prue's flat in South Kensington — she shares with another girl — and I got some of the story out of her. Frodsham was alone in the house that evening — his mother and the manservant were out. His mother returned soon after half past ten, went into the library, and found him dead in his chair and shot through the heart. Jules — the manservant — got in a few minutes later and telephoned to the police. And Prue arrived as usual at ten o'clock the next morning and walked into a house full of French mourning and constabulary.

"Well, now we come to the real trouble. Prue wouldn't open up at all, but I saw she was frightened, and I questioned her rather hard. Finally she admitted that she had gone back to Richmond in the evening and had been seen by someone outside Frodsham's house. She says she didn't go into the house, and she's speaking the truth." Tim met Johnny's eyes steadily. "I know that, even if the police don't. But she won't tell me why she went back or what she did do, so how can I help her?" He looked intolerably unhappy and all at once pathetically young. "I'd have told you about it this morning if you'd been at the shop, Johnny. I want her to talk to you, and she said she might — perhaps. But she wanted to think it over, so she wouldn't let me see her today. She said I could ring her up this evening."

There was a long silence. Then Johnny said slowly: "I can't do anything unless she does talk to me, Tim. And even if she does, I may not be able to help. Sally and I have solved two murders, as you know, but more by luck than by good guidance. Still, if she'll talk, I'll do what I can. By the way, where are her people? Aren't they taking an interest?"

"They're somewhere in the Pacific," said Tim. "They're cruising to New Zealand and Australia by way of Panama. They won't be back for quite a long time, unless they hear about this, and I hope to God they won't. They'd do far more harm than good." He hesitated a moment, and then added: "Thanks, Johnny."

* * *

Tim allowed himself to be persuaded to stay for tea, but he was very restless. When they had finished, his patience gave way suddenly, and he said he was going to ring up Prue's flat. He was answered but evidently not by Prue. He listened for a minute or two, frowning heavily, and then said: "All right, Clare. I'm coming back now — I'm in Sussex at the moment. I'll be with you soon after six. If she comes back don't let her go out again before I get there."

He turned to Johnny and Sally. "That was Prue's stable-companion," he said. "Prue left the flat about half past one, and she hasn't been back. She wouldn't tell Clare where she was going."

"Did she take any luggage with her?" asked Johnny.

"No. So she hasn't panicked and run away. That wouldn't be like her anyway. I'm going back to town now, and I shall wait at the flat till she comes. Will you come with me, Johnny?"

"Very well," said Johnny. "I'll come—" He broke off. Someone was knocking on the front door.

"Oh my God!" said Tim with a sharpness which betrayed his raw nerves.

"Come upstairs with me," said Johnny calmly. "I must change. Sally will deal with it."

The box-stair opened off the sitting room. Sally saw them disappear as she went to the front door.

She had expected one of their country neighbours whom they were beginning to know. But a completely strange girl stood on the doorstep — a girl with a small pale face framed in a head-square. She said gravely: "Please forgive me, but is this Thatchers?"

"Yes?" said Sally, questioningly.

"I think you must be Mrs Heldar. I'm Prudence Thorpe. I think perhaps Tim's spoken of me."

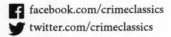